I am not one of the beautiful people.

Some people are born with everything—looks, personality, brains. Any combination of two can usually get you by. You might not be much to look at, but if you're a fun person and are smart, you'll be fine. If you're beautiful and personable, you could have oatmeal between your ears and no one would care much. But these natural laws that govern the social universe all fall apart when your looks are like a black hole. That's me: a freakish blip in time and space—a singularity of ugliness. An *ugularity*—and no matter how smart I am, no matter how friendly or funny, it doesn't matter. All that's good about me gets sucked in and crushed into nothing when the world looks at me.

I could have accepted my fate, doomed to be an ugularity for my entire life, but then one day I was given the chance to trade in this face for all time. Who wouldn't choose that if they could? No matter how unspeakable the consequences . . .

OTHER SPEAK BOOKS

Duckling Ugly

NEAL SHUSTERMAN

darkfusion   ▲   BOOK 3

Duckling Ugly

speak

An Imprint of Penguin Group (USA) Inc.

SPEAK

Published by the Penguin Group

Penguin Group (USA), Inc., 345 Hudson Street, New York, New York 10014, U.S.A.

Penguin Group (Canada), 90 Eglinton Avenue East, Suite 700, Toronto, Ontario, Canada M4P 2Y3
(a division of Pearson Penguin Canada Inc.)

Penguin Books Ltd, 80 Strand, London WC2R 0RL, England

Penguin Ireland, 25 St Stephen's Green, Dublin 2, Ireland
(a division of Penguin Books Ltd)

Penguin Group (Australia), 250 Camberwell Road, Camberwell, Victoria 3124, Australia
(a division of Pearson Australia Group Pty Ltd)

Penguin Books India Pvt Ltd, 11 Community Centre,
Panchsheel Park, New Delhi - 110 017, India

Penguin Group (NZ), Cnr Airborne and Rosedale Roads, Albany, Auckland 1310, New Zealand
(a division of Pearson New Zealand Ltd)

Penguin Books (South Africa) (Pty) Ltd, 24 Sturdee Avenue,
Rosebank, Johannesburg 2196, South Africa

Registered Offices: Penguin Books Ltd, 80 Strand, London WC2R 0RL, England

First published in the United States of America by Dutton Children's Books,
a division of Penguin Young Readers Group, 2006
Published by Speak, an imprint of Penguin Group (USA), Inc., 2007

1 3 5 7 9 10 8 6 4 2

Copyright © Neal Shusterman, 2006

THE LIBRARY OF CONGRESS HAS CATALOGED THE DUTTON EDITION AS FOLLOWS:

Shusterman, Neal.
Duckling ugly / by Neal Shusterman.
p. cm.
Summary: When sixteen-year-old Cara, a girl ugly enough to break mirrors,
is drawn to a place where everyone can be beautiful,
her deepest desire is to return home to say goodbye—and get revenge.
[1. Ugliness—Fiction. 2. Beauty, Personal—Fiction. 3. Revenge—Fiction.
4. Supernatural—Fiction.] I. Title.
PZ7.S55987Du2006   [Fic]—dc22   2005010661

Speak ISBN 978-0-14-240684-7

Designed by Jason Henry

Printed in the United States of America

PART ONE

▲

"UGULaRITY"

I am not one of the beautiful people.

Some people are born with everything—looks, personality, brains. Any combination of two can usually get you by. You might not be much to look at, but if you're a fun person and are smart, you'll be fine. If you're beautiful and personable, you could have oatmeal between your ears and no one would care much. But these natural laws that govern the social universe all fall apart when your looks are like a black hole. That's me: a freakish blip in time and space—a singularity of ugliness. An *ugularity*—and no matter how smart I am, no matter how friendly or funny, it doesn't matter. All that's good about me gets sucked in and crushed into nothing when the world looks at me.

This is what the world sees when it dares to look:

A pair of sewer-shade eyes two sizes too big for my face; a weak chin with a spidery mole. Hair like brown weed-whacked crabgrass, and a flat chest over shapeless hips. It's worse when I smile, because my brother got all the good teeth. Braces were always out of the question.

As I once overheard my dentist say to his assistant, "Braces on *that* girl would be like lipstick on a horse."

The word is *ugly.* Oh, there are other words for it. Words like *plain,* you know? Like vanilla. But if I were ice cream, I'm sure I'd be broccoli- or cabbage-flavored.

I could have accepted my fate, doomed to be an ugularity for my entire life, but then one day I was given the chance to trade in this face for all time. Who wouldn't choose that if they could? No matter how unspeakable the consequences. . . .

1

TO THE BONE

I will always remember the lights, stark and hot, shining on me from every angle. They exposed my face for the whole world to see. Being onstage in front of hundreds of people should have been a high point of my life, but those lights . . . I felt naked beneath them. My pores had opened—I could feel sweat running down my face, coursing around zits and moles like boulders in a river, then pouring down my neck, to soak the collar of my blouse. I knew even before we began that things were going to go wrong.

"Contestant number thirteen," the head judge said, his voice booming into the microphone. "Cara DeFido."

I stood up. There were hundreds of people in the audience. I couldn't see them, but I did hear whispers. I tried to make myself believe they weren't whispering about me.

"Spell the word *unprepossessing.*"

That's an easy one, I thought. There was a little tittering from certain members of the audience when he said the word, but I didn't let it get to me.

"Unprepossessing." I said. "*U-N-P-R-E-P-O-S-S-E-S-S-I-N-G.* Unprepossessing."

"That's correct."

There was some halfhearted applause as I sat back down.

Everyone's good at something. I can spell. I guess it's just an inborn ability—something to do with the way my brain is wired. It's the kind of skill that goes unnoticed except at spelling bees. Kids can win thousands of dollars at the national level. "There's a market for every skill," my dad says, "even the weird ones." So once a year I get to go up onstage for the county spelling bee, and I always win it. I never go on to the state or national spelling bees, though. I could, but I don't. Those bigger contests are televised; I got my reasons for not getting in front of cameras.

As I sat there and waited for my next turn, the word I had just spelled stuck in my throat like a pill, just dissolving there, tasting bitter.

Unprepossessing.

It was another one of those nice words for "ugly." Even nicer than *plain*. It was just a coincidence that the judge's computer came up with that word for me to spell, but still it bothered me. Momma would have called it ironic. The Almighty showing He's got Himself a sense of humor. I'm sure that's what she was thinking out there in the audience.

Well, she's not me. The contests she went out for when she was my age were beauty contests, not spelling bees. She was possessing, *pre*possessing—there was no "un" about it.

"Contestant thirteen," the judge's voice boomed.

In the previous round, there had been five more eliminations. Only six of us remained. I stood up and felt the searing spotlight on me again.

The judge looked at the word that had been thrown up on his

computer screen, and he hesitated. He glanced at the judge next to him, who only shrugged. He took a deep breath and turned to me.

"Please spell *abomination.*"

Some gasps of surprise from the audience. A few snickers.

The heat I felt in my ears, then cheeks had nothing to do with the lights. I knew I was going blotchy red. I tried to tell myself it was just coincidence again, but deep down I knew it wasn't. This word was too easy. The other kids were getting words like *cairngorm* and *pneumonectomy*. Whether this was the Almighty having a major laugh or something other, I couldn't figure out yet.

"Abomination," I said. "*A-B-O-M-I-N-A-T-I-O-N*. Abomination."

"Correct."

I sat back down and looked at the crack-nail toes sticking through the tips of my sandals.

There's that old joke: "Beauty is only skin deep, but ugly goes right to the bone." But they're wrong—because with me it goes deeper than the bone. It goes right to the marrow. I once overheard our pastor say to one of the other parishioners that looking at me was enough to question your belief in God. Momma overheard it, too, so we left that church and found another.

Four more contestants were disqualified, one after another. It was down to me and some brainiac who kept nervously cracking his knuckles.

"Contestant thirteen," came the booming voice.

I stood.

When the judge looked at the computer screen this time, he took his time. He called all the other judges over. They conferred, then sat down again, looking back and forth to one another. When the head judge got on the microphone, he didn't offer me a word to spell. He offered me his apologies.

"I'm sorry, Miss DeFido . . . but the rules are very strict," he said. "We have no choice but to give you the word that comes up on the screen. You understand?"

I nodded.

"There's nothing we can do about it."

I nodded.

He took a deep breath and said, "Please spell . . . *grotesque.*"

And this time there was unrestrained laughter in the audience; the chuckling, twittering voices of students, and parents, too. This was no accident. Somewhere out there, I knew, there was one kid, or two, or a whole gaggle of them who were secretly gloating over having somehow pulled this prank.

I knew what I had to do. Holding my head as high as I could manage, I spelled the word.

"Grotesque," I said. *"G-O . . ."* I leaned closer to the microphone. *"T-O . . ."* I grabbed the microphone stand like a rock star. *"H-E . . ."* I looked out over all those people in the audience. *"L-L.* Grotesque."

Silence from the judges. Silence from the audience.

Finally, the head judge leaned toward his microphone. "Uh . . . I'm sorry," he said. "That is incorrect."

Then, in the front row, a newspaper photographer stood up and brought his camera to his eye.

Go on, take my picture, I thought. *Go on. I dare you.*

And I smiled for him, as wide as I could, stretching my lips over my terrible teeth.

The lens shattered with such force the entire camera fell to pieces.

People nearby shielded their eyes from the flying shrapnel, and the photographer, his hands and face bloody, stood for a moment staring in shock, then raced down the aisle in pain.

"Cheese," I said.

Then I took off the number 13 sticking to my shirt and left.

My mother found me walking by the side of the road ten minutes later. She pulled up in her classic pink Cadillac—the kind they got sticking out of the roof of the Hard Rock Cafe. It has wings like the Batmobile and funky bullet-shaped taillights. Everyone knows when Momma drives down the street. When she saw me, she slowed down, matching my pace.

"Cara DeFido, you get yourself into this car."

"Give me one good reason."

"Because it's a twenty-mile walk back to Flock's Rest."

"So I'll hitchhike," I told her.

"And who is it you think's gonna pick you up?"

"Yeah," said my brother from the backseat. "One look at her and they'll break the land-speed record to get away."

Momma turned around and tried to whack him, but her headrest got in the way. "You just shut that piehole, Vance," Momma said.

"Hey, I'm just trying to help!"

The way Momma saw it, she was the only one allowed to tell me how ugly I was, and she had no qualms about doing it. *"Honey,"* she used to say when I was little, *"you're as ugly as a duck-*

ling coming out of its shell." And then she would kiss all those ugly parts of my face.

It might sound horrible, but you gotta understand, she said it out of love. Okay, maybe a little out of bitterness, too, but mostly out of love. See, my momma, she's smart enough to know there's some things the world doesn't forgive. The world can forgive you for being stupid. It can forgive you for being blind, for being deaf; it can even forgive you for being bad. This world doesn't forgive ugliness, though—and if Momma had pretended that I wasn't, it would have been a cruelty beyond measure, because how could I ever face the world without being prepared for the nastiness it would eventually kick back at me?

I knew she couldn't be too mad at me for what I did at the spelling bee, because she had raised me not to take any guff for being ugly. Some kids need tough love—well, Momma raised me with ugly love.

Even now I could see the love behind her stern face. I knew she wanted to jump out of that car, hug me, and make all the meanness in the world go away. But just as she wouldn't give me that hug, I wouldn't ask for it. We both understood that sympathy was one step above pity, and we would have none of that.

"I don't like what happened in there any more than you do," Momma said, "but if you think I'm gonna let you walk home, you got something else coming!"

"I swear, Momma, if you make me get in that car, I will look into your rearview mirror, and your side mirrors, too!"

"So what?" said Momma. "I'll just buy new ones, and take it out of your allowance."

"What allowance?"

By now Momma's patience had worn as thin as her mascara. "Cara, I am not gonna say it again. Get in this car!"

I looked at the road before me. It was straight, the ground was flat, and in the distance, I could see the mountains. Our town was at the base of those mountains. It was getting late in the afternoon, but I didn't care if it got dark. I could probably be home by midnight if I walked fast enough. Then I saw the billboard about a hundred yards ahead, featuring my father's smiling face, before his hair went salt-and-pepper. It was one of the really old billboards back from the days when he had a dozen used-car lots around the county, instead of just one. DEFIDO MOTORS, the billboard said. WE TREAT YOU RIGHT-O AT DEFIDO. The sign was faded, but it didn't stop his face from looking down on me. I wondered how many of these old billboards were on the road between here and home. I could bear a twenty-mile walk, but not the prospect of Dad glaring down at me ten times larger than life, over and over again.

"Did you call Dad?" I asked Mom.

"And tell him what? That you spelled a four-letter word?"

"Technically," said Vance, "it was one four-letter word, and a couple of two-letter words."

"I had every right to do it!"

Mom didn't answer right away. She just kept that stern expression, then said, "Maybe you did, but it doesn't mean I have to like it."

Then another car passed, heading back toward Flock's Rest, and one of my classmates shouted out the window, "Hey, DeFido, wha'cha doing there? I don't see no sign that says COYOTE CROSSING!"

There was laughter from the other kids in the car, and they peeled out.

Momma pursed her lips and ignored it, the way she always taught me to ignore it—but I think it hurt her more than it hurt me.

"If you walk, you'll have nothing but your own thoughts for company," she said. "And some evil company they'll be. The sooner we get you home, the sooner you can get your thoughts on something else."

"Ah, she'll just go into her room and do some more of those stupid ink drawings," said Vance. Momma gave him her best dirty look, and he wilted like a fern in a frost.

In the end, I got into the car. Not because of the long walk, not even because of having to face my dad's billboards. It was that passing car that made me realize I couldn't make the walk . . . because I knew everyone riding back to Flock's Rest from the spelling bee would pass me, and I couldn't bear the thought of every single driver having something to say.

2

master-means

I touched the tip of the wolf-hair brush to the surface of the ink and watched as the ink slowly wicked up into the brush, until it shone wet and dark.

At first I didn't know what had drawn me to Chinese ink painting. I didn't even know anyone Chinese. There was something about the simplicity of it, and the feel of a single bamboo brush carving up the white void. It just felt right. Then I learned that the art form began as a way to write the complicated symbols of the language. It all made sense to me then. Ink drawing was the Chinese version of spelling! I even went as far as to learn the seven basic strokes of Chinese writing and use only those strokes in the things I drew, so it all had a mysterious Zen look about it.

I wasn't a master artist or anything, but that didn't matter. I didn't draw for others. I did it because of how it made me feel. I could lose myself in those brushstrokes—and as my brother had so rudely guessed, that's exactly what I did when I got home from the spelling bee.

My favorite subject to draw was "Nowhere Valley," or at least that's what I called it. You see, there are two places I like to go when the outside world becomes too cruel. Nowhere Valley is one of them. It exists only in my head: a hidden place of rolling hills covered in hundreds of shades of green. I imagine myself walking along a meandering stone path, breathing in the smells of wildflowers and orange blossoms. People wave to me from their pastel-colored houses as I pass, and I wave back. I hear voices filled with joyous laughter, not mocking laughter. Sometimes I see the valley in my dreams, but more often I see it in my daydreams. My simple brush drawings can almost capture the essence of the place. I wouldn't dare add color, because there's no pigment in the world that could do justice to what I see in my mind. Adding color would be sacrilege—like colorizing a classic old movie.

Today, however, my heart was not in my brush. No matter how I drew the hills and paths, my imaginary valley gave me no comfort. So I rinsed off my brush, capped the ink, and decided to visit that second place I go to when life gets the better of me. It was the only place I knew where the residents didn't care how ugly you were. That's because they were dead.

"Vista View" has to be the worst name ever given to a cemetery. First of all, the word *vista* already means "view" in Spanish, so the name is really "View View." And second, when you're six feet under, you've got no view, except for maybe your own toes, so pointing out the beautiful view is kind of insulting to the dead, don't you think?

Vista View hasn't always been a cemetery. Back in the day, it was a botanical garden—the most beautiful in the state. Winding trails and beautiful trees and flowers from all over the world filled the place. Our town of Flock's Rest got its name because of Vista View. Flocks of all kinds of birds would make their trek over the mountains and be drawn to the lush greenery of the botanical garden, where they'd fill the trees and ponds, making a racket that could be heard for miles. The woman who owned the place entertained bird-watchers in her little white house on a hill, smack in the middle.

But then the place went bankrupt. An undertaking conglomerate bought it and decided it was a fine place to plant people instead of trees. Now rich people from all over bury their loved ones there, paying more for a little burial plot than most people pay for homes. The beautiful trees and stuff are still there—only now those winding paths are all lined with gravestones. As for the old woman, they let her stay on in her house, but I don't know if I'd want to live in the middle of dead people, no matter how nice the view-view was.

I told my parents I was taking a nap, then I locked my bedroom door and climbed out of the window. I was careful to slip out the back way of our mobile-home park so they wouldn't see me. Let my parents think I was brooding in my bed, wallowing in self-pity. They didn't need to know everything I did.

It was dusk when I got there. It was the time of day when the colors of the earth bow out and let the colors of the sky take over. This was my favorite time of day, because shadows get long, and with a face like mine, shadows are your friend.

There was a strange smell in the graveyard today. Something chemical that I couldn't place at first. Then, when I heard the metallic rattle followed by a long smooth *hissss,* I knew what that smell was. Spray paint.

I heard their voices just in time and ducked behind a tall gravestone. Cautiously, I peered out of the shadows to see them.

Marshall Astor shook the spray can in his hand, then dotted the *I*'s and crossed the *T*'s of something nasty he had sprayed on a gravestone.

Lately the gravestones had been smashed and defaced by kids too stupid to find something better to do with their time. I hated it, because spraying rudeness on tombstones was the opposite of what I did with brush and ink.

I should have known Marshall Astor was the one who'd been doing it. And sitting right beside him on a little stone mourner's bench was Marisol Yeager, his partner in crime. They were the undisputed king and queen of Flock's Rest High. He was handsome, she was gorgeous, the world smiled on them, and they smiled right back. The way I see it, when you've got those kind of looks you have a choice: You can either use the brains God gave you, or you can skate through life on your looks and never let your brain develop much beyond dog intelligence. Marisol and Marshall had chosen the latter.

"Ooh, this place is so spooky," Marisol said. "I love it."

Marshall went on to another grave and shook his spray can, preparing for another round of vandalism.

"Can I try?" Marisol asked.

"Okay," Marshall said. "But you got to think up something clever to write."

Marshall Astor was rumored to be distantly related to the famous Astors—you know, the rich ones who went down on the

Titanic. If it was true, then some other distant cousins must have gotten all the money and class. Still, it had never stopped Marshall's father from wearing the name like he was royalty—that is, until the day he had too much to drink, drove off a bridge into the river, and went down with the Buick.

Marshall was half as smart and twice as useless as his father ever was—but he was strong, had a winning smile, and good hair in a stiff wind. Around here, that's enough to make you mayor, which his father was until that fateful day.

"How about this?" said Marisol, still pondering what to spray on the tombstone. "'Why do I always wake up with dead hair.' Get it? 'Dead hair'?"

Make that fly intelligence. Marisol had always been one of those baby beauty queens, with platinum blond hair that had probably been bleached from birth. Our hatred of each other was deeply ingrained, but I'll get to that later.

These two were the source of much misery around Flock's Rest High. They were what I call *master-means*. Not master "minds," because that would be giving them too much credit— but they did have a way of motivating other people to do their thinking for them.

As Marisol sprayed her message on a nearby gravestone, I tried to figure out how I could get out of there without being noticed. It wasn't dark enough yet to escape unseen, and I wasn't quiet enough to slip away unheard. But maybe if I waited, the shadows would take over and I could scurry away before they started the make-out session that I knew was coming. Maybe the sound would startle them enough to make them leave and go swap saliva somewhere else, which was fine by me.

But before I could plan a suitable getaway, Marisol came around the tombstone, looking for another one to spray, and saw me lurking there. She let out a scream that could wake the dead around us.

I jumped back at that ear-piercing shriek, hitting a tree—but when I turned, I saw it wasn't a tree at all. It was Marshall, who stood there like an oak.

"Well, look what we have here," he said. "Nothing to be scared of, Marisol. It's just the Flock's Rest Monster."

I grimaced at the nickname. It had been with me for as long as I could remember.

My grimace must have looked like a wolf baring its teeth, because he said, "Look at that, I think it's got rabies."

"What do you think you're doing," Marisol said, "spying on people?"

"I wasn't spying, I was just—"

"You're sick," Marshall said.

"No, no, what was the word?" Marisol said slowly. "She's an . . . *abomination*!"

That caught me off guard. Had they been there that day—or had they only heard? Or were they the master-means behind it?

I lunged toward Marisol, wanting to rip that pretty skin off her face, but Marshall held me back and then tossed me against a gravestone so hard it almost toppled over. I felt the impact of that stone in every joint of my body.

"Don't you touch Marisol," he said. "You ain't got a right to touch her. Or me. Or anybody."

I tried to get away, but he pushed me back against the stone again. "Where you going, piggy girl? Don't you want to spy on us some more? Maybe I'll get you a camera. Hey, will it break if you're the one snapping the picture, too?"

Then something swung out of nowhere and slammed against Marshall's ear. He stumbled back.

Suddenly there, in the half-light of day's end, was a woman who had to be at least ninety years old, brandishing the blunt end of a pitchfork.

I knew who it was right away. Most folks just called her "the crazy woman of Vista View" and left it at that, but I knew her name: Miss Leticia Radcliffe. She was the one who lived in the house. The one who didn't leave when the place became a cemetery.

"Hey!" yelled Marshall, holding his ear. "What are you, nuts?!"

"You stay back or I'll swing it again. And next time I'll use the business end."

And, just to make her point, she swung the blunt end one more time. It didn't come anywhere near him. In fact, she wasn't even facing him directly when she swung it, and I wondered why.

"Marshall, let's just go," begged Marisol. "That witch'll kill you soon as look at you."

But Marshall was not the kind of guy to back down from a fight, especially with a feeble old woman. He stepped forward, sticking his chest out.

"You get outta here," he said to Miss Leticia. "Go on back to your house. This ain't none of your business."

"This used to be my land," she said, "so I make everything that happens here my business. You leave this girl alone, and get out the way you came."

"And if we don't?"

Then Miss Leticia Radcliffe did the most wonderful, wicked, unbelievable thing I'd ever seen. She took that old pitchfork and jammed it right through the tip of Marshall's left Nike!

Marshall wailed in pain. "Ahhh, my toe!"

Then the old woman leaned close to him and whispered, "Next time . . . it'll be your heart."

She pulled out the pitchfork, and the fight blew out of Marshall like he was a balloon that had been popped. He took off with Marisol, limping and moaning all the way.

When they were gone, Miss Leticia turned to me—and now I could see why she hadn't looked right at Marshall when she had swung that pitchfork. Miss Leticia had cataracts as gray as an April storm. She could see enough to tell night from day, I guessed, but not a whole lot more. She must have known Vista View like the back of her hand, and she didn't need to see much to know what was going on when she got there.

She looked toward me, but not quite at me. "Now I'm just guessing, mind you—but from what that boy called you, I would say that you're the DeFido girl."

"Cara," I told her. "So you heard about the nickname."

"Oh, believe me, I've been called a whole lot worse than that." She let loose a long, hearty laugh. "'The Flock's Rest Monster' ain't all that bad, considering. It sounds legendary. Dignified."

She planted the pitchfork firmly on a grave and took my hand. "You come on in. I'll make us some tea."

3

THE SWEET
AND THE RANCID

Although I didn't actually know her before that day, Miss Leticia had always been of interest to me. Maybe it was because she was an outcast in town, rumored to have killed her husband when he sold this land, which had been in her family for generations. That was long before I was born, but the rumors still hung like sheets on a clothesline, twisting more and more the longer they stayed in the wind.

Her whole life now was spent in her cottage, and the huge greenhouse behind it that had once been the centerpiece of the botanical garden. It was a grand Victorian greenhouse, with a high crystalline dome, and smaller wings on either side.

She didn't take me to the cottage—instead she took me right to the greenhouse, which was even more spectacular inside than out. Strange black orchids grew from the dark soil, and up above hung carnivorous pitcher plants so big they could drown a rat. I took a deep whiff. Every inch of the place was alive with aromas. Turn your head and the scent would change to something else.

"Being as I can't quite see the things I grow anymore," she told me, "I cultivate things that appeal to the other senses." The greenhouse was full of flowers that not only smelled sweet, but were soft to touch as well. Some of the plants grew exotic berries that danced on your tongue when you tasted them. I could see Miss Leticia more clearly in the greenhouse lights now. She was a heavy woman, but she wore her weight well. She had skin like dark chocolate, and her hair was a mess of steel wool pulled into a bun.

She led me to a little cast-iron table and chairs surrounded by staghorn ferns and lilies, but she walked a little too close and banged her shin against one of the chairs with a nasty *clang*. I grimaced, practically feeling it myself.

"You all right?" I asked.

"Yep. It wasn't me anyway—it was this thing." She lifted her skirt a bit to reveal steel braces that ran up either side of her shin, practically up to her knee. She had them on both legs. "Metal on metal—that's why it sounded so loud. I got steel rods in my back, too—and a pacemaker. Got a grandson calls me Nana Cyborg, on accounta all that metal." She laughed so contagiously, I had to laugh, too. "Then, after all that, I got these cataracts in my eyes, and I said, 'No more!' There'll be no more doctors touching this here body less'n it's to pretty it up for my wake." She laughed again. It seemed strange that she could joke so easily about dying, but then, when you're as old as Miss Leticia, death stops being the enemy.

"Now you just sit yourself down, and I'll go get that tea," she said. She went off into her cottage and returned a few minutes later with a tray.

"It's good to have a guest," she told me. "No one comes around but my son and that horrible wife of his. And all *they* want to talk about is putting me in a home. But I tell them I got a home."

I breathed in the steam of her tea, then took a gentle sip. Although her cloudy gray eyes had been disturbing at first, after I'd been sitting and drinking with her for just a few minutes, any sense of discomfort faded away. "Now you tell me your troubles," she said, "because my guess is you got no one else worth tellin' em to."

"I just had a bad day, is all." I didn't say anything more, hoping I wouldn't have to get into it—but Miss Leticia wasn't going to let me off the hook.

"Hmm," she said when she realized I wasn't talking. Then she rapped her knuckles against one of her leg braces. "These braces here give me support. I don't mind, on account of I know my legs need it—otherwise they hurt something awful. I know you're hurting as well. Ain't no shame in needing a little support." She took a long, slow sip of her tea. "Now, why don't you tell me what happened that's got you so upset?

"Clammed up, are ya? Hmm. Must be a lot going on in that head of yours."

Then she smiled a little too mischievously for a woman of her age. "What could it hurt to let some steam out of that pressure cooker?"

I sighed. "Well, I was in this spelling bee, and—"

"Ah," she interrupted, "I knew you were the type for casting spells!"

"No, not *casting* spells," I told her. "It's about spelling *words.*"

"Spells, spelling; it's all the same," she said. "Puttin' letters in order is no different than puttin' words in order. There's a magic to both of them, true enough."

Though I knew the notion was crazy, it was exciting to think that something as ordinary as spelling could have a kind of power. Maybe there was more to me than offends the eye!

When I told her about the words I'd been forced to spell, she pursed her lips and said, "My, my, my, what a place we live in. I think the people around this town are just unnaturally cruel."

"No," I told her. "People are the same everywhere, whether it's here in Flock's Rest or in some other town. They take one look at me, and they just can't control the things they say and do."

Miss Leticia waved her hand. "Don't you give no mind to the things people say. It's just a whole lotta quacking from a whole lotta geese."

"Yeah," I said, "but what about the things they *do*?"

Miss Leticia didn't have a quick answer for that one. "All I can say about that is what goes around comes around. You may never get to see it, but those kids who played that evil trick on you today, they will get theirs. And if it's not in this world, it will be in the next."

She said it with such certainty, it made me feel better. After that, I began talking about everything, as though a floodgate had opened inside of me. I went on and on about the things people said about me—to my face and behind my back. I told her about how most strangers treated me—as if touching me would somehow make them unclean. I even told her things about my parents that I'd never told anyone. Like how years ago, when my momma was sick, my dad had to take me to work with him. I spent a week with him on the car lots, and that was the week people stopped buying his cars.

"Within a year, all of his lots, except for one, went out of business, and we had to move to a trailer park. We've been there ever since. He never said it out loud, but I know he blames me. He thinks my face cursed his business."

"Hmm," said Miss Leticia. "Tell me, is your father an honest salesman?"

"Not really," I admitted. "His cars are mostly pieces of garbage."

"Well, then, his business deserved to be cursed."

I told her about my ink drawings, and the green valley I go to in my mind, where the people don't seem to notice my face—and how the flowers of her greenhouse reminded me of the gardens I imagine there.

"Tell me, child—do you sleepwalk?"

I hesitated. First, because it was an odd question, and second, because I wasn't quite sure how I wanted to answer. "No," I finally said.

"All right, then. I had thought that maybe the place you was seeing is real, and maybe it was calling to you. That happens, you know."

I was going to tell her about the problem I had with mirrors and cameras, but I stopped myself—maybe because I was afraid to hear what she might say.

"You talk about being so ugly," Miss Leticia said. "I wish I could see you to tell you that you're not. But all I see these days are shadows, like I'm lookin' through a shower curtain."

"That's all right," I told her softly. "If you saw me, you probably wouldn't even let me in here."

She laughed at that. "Is that how little you think of me?"

I didn't answer her. I knew now that Miss Leticia was a great soul, but there were some things I didn't think even a great soul could stand.

"Come here, Cara. I want to show you something."

Then Miss Leticia took my hand and led me through the greenhouse to a far corner. We pushed our way through a row of dense, lacy ferns to see the strangest growing thing I'd ever seen.

It was a pod, about three feet high, with a fat stalk pushing its way out of the top.

"Now tell me what you think this is," Miss Leticia said with a smirk.

"I have no idea."

"It comes from the rain forests of Sumatra. That stalk will grow six feet before it opens up into a flower. Take a deep whiff."

I did, but all I could smell were the sweet blooms growing elsewhere in the greenhouse.

"I don't smell it."

"No, not yet, but you will." She reached over and gently brushed her hand along the smooth stalk like it was a beloved pet. "I've been nursing this one for years, and this is the first time it's going to bloom. The Titan Arum, it's called . . . but some folks call it the Corpse Flower. You know why?"

I shook my head.

"It's called that," she told me, "because when it blooms, it smells like the rotting dead."

I shuddered at the thought. "I guess the cemetery's the perfect place for it, then," I said nervously. Why on Earth, with all the wonderful-smelling plants she had, would she choose to grow this thing?

She must have read my mind because she said, "Oh, the scent of roses and gardenias is fine, but everyone needs a break from all that cloying perfume. Now and again I treasure the scent of something . . . other."

I took in another breath, trying to imagine what the flower would smell like once it bloomed, but I guess my imagination wasn't pungent enough.

"The beautiful and the terrible, the sweet and the rancid—it's all part of God's glory and has its reason to be," Miss Leticia said. "Just like you, Cara."

Suddenly she grabbed my wrists so tightly I could feel her nails cutting into my skin. "You have a destiny, child," she said. "Don't let anyone tell you that you don't."

Then she looked at me, and I swear she could see me through the deadness of her cataracts. "You came to me in your dark time, confiding in me, and that binds us," she said. "And so I will make it my business to be there when your destiny comes calling."

All the way home, I felt the sting of Miss Leticia's nails. I knew her nail marks would be in my forearms for days—but I didn't mind.

You have a destiny, she had said. Those marks were a reminder.

Miss Leticia was weird, but she was wise in a way few people could understand. Whether she knew things or just suspected things, I didn't know—but then, to a person with intuition, suspicion had to count for something. No one had ever suggested I had a place and a purpose in the world. My parents, who on their best days saw life as an inconvenience, had never—*could* never—make me feel the way Miss Leticia had in the short time I had known her.

It was around 9:30 at night when I climbed back through my

bedroom window. My parents were always respectful of my privacy, so I don't think they even knew I'd been gone. They probably just thought I'd wallowed myself to sleep—as if self-pity was some kind of narcotic.

Well, okay, maybe I did feel a little sorry for myself, but that never made me want to wallow in misery. It just made me mad. It made me want to do something about it, if only I could find the right thing to do. The *satisfying* thing to do.

I opened my door to the fading smell of fried chicken. Dinner was over, but I knew there would be a plate in the fridge for me. My chicken would have its skin peeled off, because Momma had heard that oily foods make acne worse, so what she serves me always has the flavor and consistency of hospital food.

Mom was in her bedroom, probably reading a self-help book; Vance was in his room listening to music so loud I could hear which song was playing in his earphones; and Dad was in the living room, drinking a beer and watching RetroToob, the cable network devoted completely to old, goofy TV shows he grew up with.

I quietly closed my door again, not hungry for dinner or family time. Instead I turned to face my dresser and played the game I played every night. It's called Does Cara Have the Nerve? See, there's this big old mirror attached to my dresser. I've never actually looked into it because it's covered with a sheet, just like most of the other mirrors in our house. I hear in some places it's a custom to cover mirrors with a sheet when you're in mourning, and I wonder sometimes if my parents are in mourning for the beautiful daughter they never had. Anyway, my momma won't let me get rid of the mirror because it's part of a set. So, just to tick her off, I glued a bunch of ugly things on the sheet covering the mirror: a baboon's butt, a dentist's image of advanced tooth decay, plastic vomit. Momma says I have a twisted sense of humor, but at least I have one.

My heart was racing that night, though, because I thought that this might be the night I win the game. This could be the day I actually defied her, and everyone else in this hateful town, by tempting fate and looking into that mirror.

I took a step closer to the dresser. My conversation with Miss Leticia had made me feel strong, purposeful. That's a good word, P-U-R-P-O-S-E-F-U-L. Spelling it even made me feel more so. I reached up my hand, and took another step closer.

D-E-T-E-R-M-I-N-E-D.

My words gave me power. They made me feel that I could change the way things had always been. That I could pull off the sheet, look myself in the face, and the mirror would hold the reflection, just like it did for other people. For *normal* people. My fingertips were against the sheet now.

V-I-C-T-O-R-I-O-U-S.

But who was I kidding? I knew what would happen. The mirror would see me and shatter, just like every mirror.

A-G-O-N-I-Z-I-N-G.

And then I would have to explain to Mom and Dad exactly what had possessed me to destroy this lovely piece of furniture.

A-B-O-R-T.

In the end, my courage failed me. My words failed me. I pulled my hand back from the sheet and let it be. The game was lost. Tonight was not the night—but I refused to feel miserable about it. Mom with her helpless self-help books, and Dad with his TV nostalgia, had misery wallowing down to an art—but I refused to join them . . . because, as Miss Leticia had said, *I have a destiny.*

I just had to figure out what it was.

4
THE MERCY SEAT

That night—the night before I received the mysterious letter—I had a dream.

It was a driving dream—I'd had a lot of those since Mom had taught me to drive a few months before. I was behind the wheel of her big old pink Caddie, and we were driving down a highway, heading out of Flock's Rest.

"Just keep your eyes on your destination," Mom said, which didn't make sense, because I couldn't see my destination, but people don't talk sense in dreams—especially your parents.

We crossed over the river where Marshall's dad went the way of the *Titanic* and out onto a long stretch of highway.

We kept passing Dad's old, faded billboards—just like we always do in real life. WE TREAT YOU RIGHT-O AT DEFIDO, said one. BUY AT DEFIDO: SOLID CARS FROM SOLID TIMES, said another.

Those signs were put up at a time when everyone thought our family was riding a wave to better places, but instead we wiped out. Dad's biggest consolation was that the billboard company that rented the signs went out of business before his car lots began to fail—and so all those advertisements for DeFido Motors were still up. Sure they were fading and peeling, but anywhere you drove in the county, you could still see my dad's smiling face looking down on you, along with some car he had once tried to sell.

"The clock broke during my fifteen minutes of fame," Dad would say every time we passed one of those old billboards.

In the dream, though, we came up on the billboards much more often than in real life. The next one featured Mom's Cadillac. I remembered seeing it before on one of the roads heading north out of town.

"Look, there's us!" Mom said in the dream. "Wave hello!"

We passed the billboard, and then I heard a different voice beside me. A younger voice.

"Shouldn't you be getting home?" the voice said. "Everyone's waiting for you."

I turned to see a boy about my age sitting next to me in the car, where my mother had been. I couldn't quite see his face—all I could see were his eyes. They were beautiful. A shade of blue that couldn't exist anywhere but in a dream.

"Who are you?" I asked.

"Better keep your eyes on the road," he said gently, but I couldn't look away from him.

"Mom, she's doing it again!"

I woke up from the dream to find myself standing in the corner of my room. The northwest corner, to be exact. As I stepped away from the corner and turned toward Vance, I could feel a stiffness in my legs that told me I had been standing there for hours.

"I haven't been doing anything," I told him. "I . . . I just thought I saw a spider, that's all."

"Yeah, sure," said Vance, shaking his head and walking away.

I wasn't lying when I'd told Miss Leticia I didn't sleepwalk— because I don't actually walk, I just stand. I'm a sleep-stander. Always in the same corner, too—and I often wondered if there was no wall there, would I still stand in the same spot, or would I be a walker after all?

Thinking about it had never yielded much, so I just accepted it as one more weird thing about me. It wasn't until much later that I began to get truly curious about it and think there might be a reason for it. But on that morning, I was as clueless as ever.

With the dream quickly fading, I dressed and went out into the kitchen. Things were back to normal, as if the spelling bee had never happened. We sat at the breakfast table, with silence punctuated by cereal crunches and "pass-the-milks," as usual.

A few years back, Momma had gotten it into her head that a healthy day begins with a family breakfast, so the four of us always sat down together in the morning, even on the days it would make us late for school.

"The occasional tardy is acceptable," Momma would say. "Starting your morning without quality time is not."

You have to understand, my momma had gone to college for two reasons. One, to get a degree in psychology. Two, to catch a successful husband destined for great things. In the end, she got neither.

At breakfast that morning, I could see Vance looking back and forth between Mom and Dad, and I could tell he was waiting for the right time to talk about something. Finally, when Dad started to push his chair back, getting ready to leave, Vance blurted it out.

"I've been thinking . . ." he began.

"That's new," I said.

Usually Vance would sneer at me when I said something like that, but he didn't. Whatever his mind was wrapped up in, it was wrapped up completely. He started biting his lower lip, making his slightly buckteeth stick out like Chuck E. Cheese.

"Thinking about what?" Dad said.

"About school and stuff. I figure, being that I'm in eighth grade and all, and that I'll be starting high school next year and all . . . I was thinking maybe I might wanna go to that Catholic high school."

"We're not Catholic," Momma reminded him calmly.

"Well, you don't have to be," Vance said. "St. Matthew's takes all types, just as long as your grades are good enough, and mine are."

"I'm not paying for a private high school," Dad said. "Nothing wrong with a public education."

By now I could tell Vance was getting antsy.

"All right, then, not St. Matthew's. What about Billington High?"

"That's twenty miles away," said Dad.

"Yeah, but their football team's ten times better than Flock's Rest High."

That caught Dad's attention. Now Momma was the one getting nervous. "You fixing to play football?"

"What if I am?" said Vance.

Dad looked at him like he'd just stepped into the Twilight Zone. That's because Vance was about as athletic as an end table. He was the star of the middle-school chess team, and I always joked with him that the only sports injury he'd ever get was carpal tunnel from lifting heavy queens. No, Vance was not fixing to play football. I knew what this was about, even if my parents did not.

"Vance just doesn't want to go to the same school as me," I announced. "He doesn't want to be the kid brother of the Flock's Rest Monster."

Vance looked down into his Apple Jacks. "That's not true," he said, but by the way he said it, you could tell it was.

"Tell you what," said Dad. "If you go out for a sport this year, make the team, *and* stay on that team for the whole season, I'll make sure you go to whatever high school you want, no questions asked."

"Yes, sir," said Vance. It was the first time I'd ever heard him call my dad "sir" outside of a spanking or grounding. He continued to stare into his Apple Jacks, probably pondering the chances that he would actually succeed.

Both Dad and Vance left that morning without ever meeting my eye . . . but what surprised me was that Momma wouldn't look at me, either.

Our school is an old brick building, with a gym that smells like sweat and varnish and a cafeteria that smells faintly of Clorox and beef gravy. It was built way back when schools were institutions, like hospitals and insane asylums. At recess I saw Marisol Yeager lingering in a downstairs hallway, surrounded by her clique of socialites. I wasn't going to give her the satisfaction of seeing me try to avoid her. I walked right past her, and she stepped in front of me.

"After last night, I'd think you'd be too ashamed to show your face in school," she said, her mouth working up and down with her usual wad of chewing gum.

I held back a smirk. I had seen Marshall limping up the steps into school this morning. It was my guess that he wouldn't tell anyone what had happened last night, because it would incriminate him as the graveyard vandal. Marisol, however, was not smart enough to keep her mouth shut.

"Don't you think I know that you and that old witch were working together?" she said. "You two are, like, in *collision* with each other."

"The word is *collusion*," I told her. *"C-O-L-L-U-S-I-O-N."*

She pursed her pretty lips angrily. Marisol hated when I spelled things for her. She had her reasons. "Here," she said. "Spell this." She raised her hand, about to flip me her favorite gesture, but before she could, I grabbed her wrist, spun her around, and wrenched her arm behind her back.

She bleated in pain, then counterattacked, stomping on my foot with her heel almost hard enough to break bones. When she pulled free, she swung her arm and hit me in the face so hard I saw stars, like in a cartoon.

I didn't want to let Marisol win, but hitting her back would just turn this into a catfight, and that simply wasn't my style. Then I realized I had a weapon that could strike at her little socialite heart. Thank goodness I had just come from art class.

I reached into my backpack and, with the dexterity of a gunslinger, took out a little bottle of drawing ink, spun off the cap, and dumped the entire thing down the front of Marisol's pretty pink designer blouse. It soaked in and spread like black blood from a wound.

She just stood there, her hands out stiff, little clicks coming from her throat instead of words.

"There," I said. "Now your outside's as black as your inside."

As I walked away she finally found her voice again, and called me every name her limited vocabulary had to offer. "You're gonna pay for this!" she yelled. "You wait and see! You're gonna pay!"

My breakfast table at home might have had every seat filled, but my lunch table at school was always empty. Some other schools have all these open-air spaces where you can go to eat lunch under a tree or something like that. They have places where you can be alone without bringing attention to the fact. We didn't have those kinds of spaces. Our cafeteria had nothing but tables for ten. Even on the occasions when I started out at a table with other kids, they always migrated elsewhere, and my table for ten became a table for one.

I would take my time eating, hogging that table for as long as I possibly could. I figured if they're not gonna sit with me, let the other tables be as cramped and uncomfortable as possible. Serves them all right.

The spot directly across from me was what I liked to call "the mercy seat." That's from the Bible. It's what they called the lid on the Arc of the Covenant, which held the Ten Commandments. The Israelite high priest would make offerings to God there. My mercy seat was a little bit different, though. See, every once in a while, someone would come and sit across the table from me. They did it out of guilt, and to feel better about themselves. They'd sit down, exchange a few awkward words with me, then go off feeling like they'd done a kind deed. They had treated the Flock's Rest Monster with a godly kind of mercy. I used to like it when people sat there, until I realized no one ever came more than once.

It had been a while since anyone had sat in the mercy seat—a month, maybe more—so I was surprised when someone came over. Today's guest was Gerardo Sanchez.

"Hey," he said as he sat down with his tray.

I just kept on eating.

"So what do you think this is?" he asked, pointing to the lumpy white stuff slithering all over an English muffin on his plate.

"Creamed gopher," I suggested. "The Tuesday special."

He chuckled. "Yeah, probably." Then he sat there in an uncomfortable silence that irked me.

"So, like, why do you sit here all by yourself?" he finally asked.

I liked his direct approach, so I answered him. "I don't sit all by myself. I just sit. Being all by myself, that's other people's idea." More silence, and so I said, "Are you gonna ask me to the homecoming dance?"

The look on his face was worth the price of admission and then some. It made me laugh out loud suddenly, and some creamed gopher came out of my nose. Seeing that made him laugh. I wiped the stuff off.

"So you weren't serious?"

"Hey," I said, "I'm serious if you are."

"Nah," he said with a certainty that left no room for doubt.

When it came to looks, Gerardo was no Marshall Astor, but he wasn't bad-looking, either. He had dark, decent hair; a body that was a little bit scrawny, but not at all mealy. His teeth had once been crooked, but braces were taking care of that. All in all, Gerardo was an average-looking guy, and from what I could see, he always had the attention of a few average-looking girls. It didn't take long for me to figure out what he was doing in the mercy seat.

"So which girl are you trying to impress?" I asked.

He gave me that openmouthed, shrug-shouldered I-don't-know-what-you-mean expression, and so I gave him that tilt-headed, cross-armed, I-ain't-buying-it look.

A moment more, and he caved. "Nikki Smith," he said with a sigh. "She thinks I'm not sensitive. I figured coming over here and talking to you might make her think different." He looked at me for another second, then began to get up. "I'm sorry," he said. "It was dumb."

On another day I might have let him go, but today I was feeling vulnerable. Although I had gotten used to being alone, some days were better than others when it came to accepting it.

"Don't leave yet," I whispered to him. "If you really want to make it stick, you have to sit here with me until the bell rings. She'll really be impressed by that."

He took on a cornered-animal look.

"Yeah, I know, sitting with me for all of lunch is a fate worse than death."

"Well, not worse," he answered, and he made himself comfortable in the mercy seat again.

"So, are you?" I asked.

"Am I what?"

"You said you wanted to show Nikki that you're sensitive. Are you?"

"I don't know. I guess." He thought about it. "I'm not *insen*sitive . . . or at least I'm not insensitive on *purpose.*"

"Well, that's better than nothing, I guess."

"Why do girls always want sensitive guys anyway?"

"They don't want their feelings hurt," I told him. "They figure a sensitive guy won't hurt their feelings, even if he breaks up with them." I noticed that Gerardo had eaten his dessert first, so I spooned my Jell-O onto his plate. A reward for taking the mercy seat. "Of course, I've got no feelings left to hurt. An insensitive guy would be fine with me, as long as I got to smack him if he got *too* insensitive."

He laughed at that, then leaned a bit closer. "So tell me, because I gotta know—how come you and Marisol hate each other so much?"

"Isn't it obvious?" I said. "Look at her, look at me."

Gerardo shook his head. "No—it's more than that. It's like you two have got . . . what's it called . . . a vendetta." *Good word,* I thought. *V-E-N-D-E-T-T-A.*

"She sat next to me in science class in seventh grade." And that was all I told him. I didn't tell Gerardo how she got by in science by copying answers from the boys she flirted with— there were always one or two within cheating distance. That particular semester she got seated in a corner with just me next to her and Buford Brainard in front of her—a kid who had all of his brains in his name, and none in his head.

So Marisol had a choice: Either she could study for the tests or cheat from me. You can guess which she chose. Up till then, Marisol's nastiness was limited to the occasional cruel jab to keep me in my place. After all, her circle was so far above mine, most of the time she didn't see me. However, things did not go well for either of us that semester, and our general feeling of dislike bloomed into something vicious.

"If you want to know why we hate each other, ask her to spell *mitochondria,*" I told Gerardo.

"Huh?"

"*Mitochondria.* Ask her to spell it."

"What'll she do if I ask?"

"Probably claw your eyes out."

"No thanks, I'll pass."

Then Gerardo looked at me—and not just a sneaky sideways glance. I get those kinds of glances all the time—people stealing a look like they might check out a circus freak. This look from Gerardo wasn't one of those, though. His eyes scanned my face, taking in all my features.

"You know, there's stuff they can do for a person's face these days," he said.

"Really?" I said. "Like what?"

"I don't know. Surgery and stuff. I saw this one show—they took a guy who was like the Elephant Man and made him look halfway decent. Not that you're the Elephant Man or anything."

He was right; he wasn't insensitive on purpose, just by accident. I could respect that. "Yeah, right, surgery," I said. "Maybe if my parents win the lottery."

"I guess that kind of thing costs an arm and a leg, huh?"

"Yeah," I said. "They charge an arm and a leg, and all they give you is a face. Pound for pound, not a very good trade, is it?"

"Guess not," he said. "But there's gotta be some guys around who'd go for a girl . . . like you."

Normally, I'd be insulted by this conversation. But Gerardo was saying it like he cared about the answer.

Suddenly Gerardo snapped his fingers. "Hey, what about that one kid, uh . . ." He looked up, trying to remember his name. "Started with a *T.* Tad. Todd."

"Tud," I said, miserably. "And that wasn't his name, it was a nickname."

"Yeah, whatever happened to him?"

"Gone," I said, and offered nothing more.

"Too bad, you two coulda been a pair."

Any inroads Gerardo had made with me were now gone. I turned my attention to my plate and didn't look up. I just scarfed down my creamed gopher.

"What? Did I say something wrong?" Gerardo asked.

I could tell him, but the telling would require an explanation, and I just didn't feel like it. "You can go now," I said. "Time off for good behavior. I'm sure Nikki will be satisfied."

"Nope, the bell hasn't rung."

I shrugged. "Suit yourself."

I didn't say another word to him.

Finally, the bell rang, he got up and left, and I knew, like all the others who had come for their own selfish reasons, he would never grace the mercy seat again.

Tud. Tuddie. A kid I hadn't thought about for more than two years, and hoped never to think about again. You could say I had blocked out his memory, but that afternoon, thanks to Gerardo, Tuddie was all I could think about as I walked home.

Tuddie was as ugly as me—maybe uglier, if you can imagine such a thing. He had ears that stuck out like fleshy funnels, a crooked underbite like a badly bred bulldog, pasty skin, and sad, sagging eyes. Like me, there was no actual physical deformity to him, he just had an unnatural case of butt-ugliness. I couldn't even remember what his real name was. Everyone just called him Tud, which was short for "That Ugly Dude."

He used to try to hang out with me when we were still in grade school, thinking we had something in common. I tried to be nice to him—I really did—but the truth was, I hated him as much as I hated the beautiful people like Marshall or Marisol. Maybe I hated Tuddie more, because he saw us as kindred spirits—as if ugliness loved company the way misery did. Well, I could live with my own face, but I didn't have to live with his. Eventually, I started ignoring him, giving him the cold shoulder, trying to be anywhere he wasn't. Still, he'd always find me—and then people started calling me Tug. "That Ugly Girl," which to me was far worse than any of the other nicknames folks gave me. "The Flock's Rest Monster"—at least that had *identity* to it. "That Ugly Girl" did not.

Finally, I snapped. I pushed that boy away—told him to crawl back under whatever rock he crawled out from, and never come out again.

And so he did.

One day he just disappeared. Some say his daddy put him out of his misery. Others say he ran away to join a freak show. Ralphy Sherman said he got sold into slavery in Madagascar. Whatever the truth was, Tuddie was gone, and I was glad for it. Once he was gone, they stopped calling me Tug and went back to calling me the Flock's Rest Monster, which was fine by me. Better a solitary monster by choice than a pathetic pair of repulsives.

But with each step I walked that afternoon, there came another memory of Tuddie's tragic, festering face, and my own sense of despair began to deepen. Looking at him was the closest I could come to looking in a mirror. His sorry fate, whatever it was, couldn't be much different from what mine would eventually be.

By the time I got home, I was feeling lower than low. The last thing I expected was to find my destiny waiting on the kitchen table.

5
question and answer

"**S**omething came in the mail for you, honey," Momma said the second I got home. She left it for me on the kitchen table, all by itself, so I couldn't miss it when I came in. It was a little white square right in the center of the big brown circle of the table.

The letter was addressed in a sweeping handwriting I couldn't imitate even if I had the finest brush. The words were like wispy clouds blowing across a windswept sky.

Miss Cara DeFido.

My name had never looked so beautiful.

"Who on earth do you think it's from?"

I just shrugged. I think Momma was more curious than I was about it. Who with such handwriting would be writing to me?

I picked up the creamy white envelope. The paper must have been expensive, soft to the touch, like velvet. I flipped it over to see who it was from, but there was no name, just an address: 1 Via del Caldero, in a city named De León.

I tried to rip the envelope open, but it wouldn't tear. I tried to peel it back from where it had been sealed, but the glue held tight.

Momma handed me her fancy letter opener. Carefully, I inserted it into the corner and slit it across. The paper resisted for a moment, then cut with no noise, as if I was cutting through a living membrane. I shivered.

"Go on, go on, see what's inside," Momma said.

I reached in and pulled out the letter. It was on the same creamy white paper. There were no marks or letterhead to reveal the sender—and only three words on the page, written in the same sweeping handwriting.

"Well, what is it?" asked Momma impatiently. "Is it a letter from someone we know? Is it an invitation?"

I held the page out of her sight.

"It's none of your business," I told her. When she realized I was serious, she huffed and left the room. Mom's curiosity would have her stewing all afternoon, but I didn't care. This, I knew, was a personal message, not meant for anyone's eyes but mine.

I sat down at the table and took a few deep breaths. I was getting light-headed, and my fingers were getting cold. An inexplicable excitement was being pumped through my veins. I looked at the smooth white note once more.

Three words. That's all. No signature, no explanation.

Those three words were a challenge, and deep in my heart, I knew it was nothing so simple or easy as a spelling bee. This was the challenge of my life.

I moved my index finger across the page, feeling its velvety smoothness, and traced the letters with my fingertip.

FIND THE ANSWERS

The three simple words that changed my life forever.

Miss Leticia's greenhouse was different during the daytime than it was at night, but it was just as beautiful. When I got there, the sun was shining through the great glass dome of its center section, casting lines across everything like the bars of a cell. I could now see the tops of the trees in the dome. To me, it was a reminder that this enclosed oasis was nothing but captured beauty. A false reality to be sure, yet easy to lose oneself in, as Miss Leticia had been lost all these years.

Today she was tending to lilies of the valley, blooming around a little indoor pond. Her hands were covered with dirt.

"They're beautiful," I told her, and then I felt bad, because I knew she couldn't really see them.

"Beautiful, yes," she said, "but poisonous as a cobra. Let me go wash my hands, and I'll make us some tea."

When she came back, I told her all about the letter.

"What do you think it means?" I asked.

Miss Leticia held the letter in her withered hands. She moved her fingers across its surface, as if it were Braille.

"My, my," she said. "This is a fine weave. Not quite paper, not quite cloth—something else." She smelled it, but I already knew it had no scent. I'm sure all she could smell was the rich aroma of all of her blooming flowers. Her prize corpse flower had not yet opened, so everything still smelled sweet and calming, like the flavor of her tea.

"Do you think it's for real?" I asked. "Or do you think it's a joke?"

"Jokes don't come on paper like this. Give me the envelope."

I put it into her hands. She rubbed her thumb on the corners.

"No stamp? Is there a postmark?"

"No."

"That means it was hand-delivered."

"Someone must have just put it into our mailbox."

"You said the town is De León?"

"Yes," I told her. "And in our state, too."

"I don't know such a place."

She handed me the letter and leaned back in her chair. As she crossed her ankles, I could hear the gentle clink of her leg braces touching each other. "I don't know where the letter came from, but I can tell you this: Whoever sent it means for you to take it very seriously. They truly mean for you to find the answers."

"How can I 'find the answers' when I don't know the questions?"

And then Miss Leticia took my hands in hers. I flinched, thinking she might grip me with her nails again, but instead she rubbed my hands gently.

"You should start with just one. What do you think the most important question is?"

I didn't answer her. Maybe because I was more afraid of knowing the question than the answer.

When I got home, Vance was fighting with Dad over the control of the living-room TV. Dad was, of course, watching RetroToob. An awful episode of the show *Nine Is Too Much,* about a huge family in the 1970s that apparently had an electronic laugh track following them wherever they went.

"How can you watch this garbage?" Vance said. "I mean, look at how they're dressed—they look like clowns."

I glanced at the TV. He was right. Striped pants and flowery shirts, all in colors that didn't match, and everyone's hair hung long in all the wrong places.

"When we were growing up," Momma said patiently, "those were the fashions. At the time it looked good to us."

Dad pointed his lecture finger at Vance. "You watch—when you have children, they're going to laugh at the way you wore your pants, and the strange things you did to your hair."

I walked past them, my hand in my pocket, still holding the mysterious note. I had no desire to be a part of the family festivities tonight.

"Honey, where have you been?" Mom asked, just noticing me.

"Out," I answered, and went toward my room, to find that my door was closed. This wasn't unusual in itself . . . but I did see something that gave me pause. There was some cloth wedged beneath my door. I recognized it as one of my sweatshirts. It was blocking the space under the door so no air could get through. Who had put it there?

I pushed open the door, and was attacked by a stench so foul, I fell back against the hallway wall.

"Oh, yuck!" I heard Vance say from the living room. "What *is* that reek?"

Holding my hand over my nose, I forced myself to enter my room. I saw it immediately. It was everywhere. Bloody masses of fur and rot tacked to my wall, all over my ink drawings.

Roadkill.

Opossums, raccoons, rabbits. It wasn't just on the walls, but in my drawers, too, every single one. It was all over my clothes, and everything I owned.

This was a violation. A horrible, evil violation of one of the few places in the world I actually felt safe from the outside world. By now Vance and my parents were at the threshold. "Honey?"

I closed the door on them. I didn't want them to see this. Roadkill in my dresser, roadkill in my closet. My clothes were ruined. Even if I could get out the smell, I'd never get out the stains. And it wasn't over yet—because there was a lump beneath my covers. A large lump. As I approached it, I steeled myself for what I might find, and before I could change my mind, I pulled back the covers.

The coyote in my bed looked like it had met up with a semi. This coyote, however, had a dog tag around its neck. And the name on the tag said: CARA DEFIDO.

I slipped out of my room, not letting my family see inside.

"Honey, what's going on in there?" Momma asked, trying to peek around me. "What's that awful smell?"

"Nothing," I told her calmly. "I'll take care of it."

"Doesn't seem like nothing to me," Dad said.

"I said I'll take care of it. Just get me some trash bags."

Like the mysterious letter, this was my business. My problem. But unlike the letter, this was no mystery. This was Marisol.

I spent the rest of that day and halfway into the night in rubber gloves, disposing of the mess and scrubbing down my room. How had things come to this? One escalation after another . . .

I should have realized she'd get revenge for her ink-stained blouse—but this was beyond a single shot of ink thrown in the heat of anger. This was premeditated, and carefully planned. She had to know when no one would be home, and she'd need accomplices to do the dirtiest of the work. How could someone so beautiful be so mean-spirited? As I scraped up nasty bits of fur, I thought back to the one and only time Marisol had been nice to me. Even then she had had an agenda.

"Cara, I know we haven't really been friends, but I think that can change."

It was seventh grade. We had just gotten pink slips to go to the principal's office. Something about cheating on a science test.

"The thing is," Marisol said, "I was sick before the test." She gave a little fake cough. "That's why I couldn't study. So I thought just this once I could borrow some answers from someone smart. Someone like you."

Then she went on to give me this whole sob story about how she was once "framed" for cheating, and if she got caught this time, the punishment would be bad.

"So what do you want me to do about it?" I asked her.

"Well, Cara," she said sweetly, "you've never been in trouble, so I figure if you admit to cheating off of me, they'll go easy on you. You just look at them with those sad eyes—how can they help but feel pity?"

"And what do I get in return?" I asked.

"My friendship," she said, "and a promise that one day I'll pay back the favor."

Ten minutes later, we were in the principal's office, and the principal told us exactly what we expected to hear, in exactly the tone of voice we expected to hear it. "Blah blah blah identical tests, blah blah blah zero tolerance." And then he waited to hear our response.

"Well," said Marisol, letting it all roll off her back, "I know nothing about this. Maybe Cara has something to say."

The principal looked at me. I took a long moment to think about this one, knowing full well what the consequences would be, either way. Finally, I said, "Every word is spelled right."

"Excuse me?" the principal said.

"The written answers. Every word is spelled right. I'm the county spelling champion, five years running." I looked at the questions on the test in front of me. Question number six was: *What do you call the engine of a human cell?* "Why don't you ask Marisol to spell *mitochondria*?"

The principal took away both tests so Marisol couldn't see. "All right, Marisol," he said. "Spell *mitochondria.*"

"Well, I don't see a reason—"

"Just do it," said the principal.

Marisol gripped her chair. First she went pale, then she started to go beet red. "Mitochondria," she said. "Mitochondria. M...I...T...O...K...O...N...D...R...Y...A."

The first time Marisol had been caught cheating she got a three-day suspension. This time she was expelled, and she spent the rest of seventh grade homeschooled.

She was back at school in the fall, though, and it had become her life's mission to make me pay.

Well, now she had. I had a trash can full of dead animals to prove it—and I knew I'd be a fool to think it would stop there.

When I was done cleaning, I took a long, hot shower, but no matter how much I scrubbed, I just didn't feel clean. I could never wash away pretty filth like Marisol Yeager, just like I could never wash away my hideous face.

I threw out my clothes. I threw out my covers. Even my mattress was ruined, so I slept on the floor that night, clutching in my hand the shimmering satin note. My one ray of hope was that letter.

Find the answers.

It seemed like a lifeline that could somehow save me from this terrible, terrible town.

6

ARE WE THERE YET?

That night I dreamed about the boy with blue eyes so intense, I couldn't see the rest of his face. I didn't know where I was at first, but as my vision cleared, I saw that we were in my special place. The green valley where all my troubles didn't seem to exist.

The boy held my hand, and we strolled down the winding stone path. His hand was soft, and the air was warm and full of wonderful floral smells, just like in Miss Leticia's greenhouse. I wished that she would appear in the dream so I could show this place to her, but she didn't.

"Are we there yet?" I asked the boy, even though I didn't know where "there" was.

"Almost," he answered. "Keep your eye on your destination."

But just as before, I couldn't. I tried to turn my head, but it seemed my eyes were locked on his. He didn't look away, the way most people do anytime I stare.

"How can you look at me?" I asked him. "I'm horrible."

He didn't answer, but he didn't look away, either. So I took the bamboo brush that had suddenly appeared in my hand and gently brushed it back and forth across my face. Instead of leaving a line of black ink, the brush erased me. I could feel my features blur into nothingness.

"There," I said. "All better now."

We kept on walking. The feeling of fury I had taken to bed was leaving me with each step down the stone path, and although this growing contentment felt wonderful, I fought to hold on to my anger. I *owned* that anger. I had earned it, and I didn't want to lose it.

I woke up standing in the northwest corner of my room.

7

BreakinG a sweat

It turns out I was wrong about Gerardo Sanchez.

I had thought he'd be just a one-lunch-stand, but he came back. Oh, he didn't come back to the mercy seat right away, but about a week later. The letter was in my pocket. I had carried it in a pocket since the day I had received it, and no matter how much I fiddled with it, it never got wrinkled or worn. I was so pleased that Gerardo actually came back to sit with me, I was going to show it to him—tell him about it, and ask him what he thought it meant—but I stopped myself. Two visits to the mercy seat wasn't enough to earn that kind of trust. And besides, Marisol might be watching. The thought of her coming by and snatching the note from my hands was enough to keep it in my pocket.

"So who are you trying to impress today?" I asked when Gerardo sat down.

"No one," he told me.

"Nikki Smith still doesn't think you're sensitive enough?"

"Yeah, she does," he said. "We're going out now. Been to the movies and everything."

"Goody for you."

There was an awkward silence, but not as bad as the first time he had sat there. "So," he asked, "what do you think's in this burger?"

I lifted my bun to reveal a gray slab beneath a sickly pickle slice. "Kangaroo," I said.

"Yeah, you can tell by the way the burgers bounce."

I looked at his plate. He wasn't touching the burger, but he had already eaten his brownie, so I gave him mine. "There. Two for the price of one."

"Thanks."

"Are you gonna tell me why you're sitting here?"

"Okay," he said, "here's the deal. If I hang out at tables with other girls, Nikki gets jealous. And if I go sit at a table with my friends, Nikki gets suspicious, thinking I'm talking about her and stuff. But she doesn't care if I sit with you. She thinks I'm being noble or something."

"Why don't you just hang out with Nikki?"

"Hey," Gerardo said, "I really like her. But it's not like I want to be around her all the time."

I knew what he meant. Nikki Smith was an okay girl, but she was also a chatterbox, and the worst kind: the kind that insisted that you respond to her chatter. She would not accept the typical "yeah . . . yeah . . . uh-huh" kind of responses that a person could usually get away with. Nikki required an in-depth analysis of every pointless thing she said, to prove you were actually listening.

"So anyway," Gerardo said, "sitting with you is like my only safe zone. Nikki doesn't get jealous because she knows there's nothing going on, and my friends don't care because it's not like I'm sitting with their enemies."

"So I'm like Switzerland," I told him.

"Huh?"

"I'm like Switzerland; I'm neutral territory."

"Yeah. Yeah, that's it."

"Only thing is," I reminded him, "Switzerland is beautiful."

"Well, to be honest, if you were beautiful, I wouldn't be sitting here with you right now, so there's something to be said for being the dog-faced girl."

I picked up my spoon and flung some peas at him, but I couldn't help but smile, because for once, someone was laughing with me, not at me.

Gerardo didn't sit with me every day after that—only when he couldn't stomach being around Nikki, which was often enough. He told Nikki he felt bad for me. He told his friends I was doing his homework for him. Neither was true. The truth was, he sat with me because he wanted to.

"I like you," he said one day. "Not in the way guys like girls, because to me you're not a girl."

I'd be lying if I said that it didn't hurt, but the hurt didn't come anywhere close to how good it felt to have him say "I like you" and know that he meant it. I could live with all the unintentional insensitivity in the world because of the unintentional honesty that came with it.

Gerardo would tell me things about himself that he couldn't tell anyone else, because unlike other kids in school, I didn't have a network of friends to gossip with. In turn, I'd tell him things, too.

One day he asked me the big question—the one he'd probably been dying to ask since that first day he took the mercy seat.

"I know it's just a stupid rumor," he began, "and I know it

couldn't possibly be true . . ." I saw how hard it was for him, so I made it easier by guessing the question myself.

"You want to know if my face breaks mirrors."

"You know what? Forget I asked," he said. "It's just a stupid thing people say—"

"It's true."

I don't think he was expecting that. He just stared at me, probably wondering if I was joking.

"Water's the only place I can see my reflection," I told him, "and even then, the water goes cloudy in a second."

"No way."

"Think about it," I told him. "The whole idea of ugly people breaking mirrors had to come from somewhere, didn't it? I'm sure it's pretty rare, but there must have been other people in history who did it."

I told him about how, when I was a baby, my father had to take out the rearview and side mirrors in our cars, because I couldn't help but look in them. "They don't have to do it anymore, since now I know better."

"That's wild!"

I guess he was right. It didn't seem wild to me, though. It's amazing the things you grow used to. "There was this one professor at the community college who tried to do a study of it," I told Gerardo. "He thought he could find some kind of scientific explanation."

"So did he?"

"Well, my mother and me went to his laboratory when I was eight. He hooked me up to wires, and computers and stuff. Then he had his assistants bring in mirrors of all shapes and sizes, on the other side of this Plexiglas barrier, and had video cameras recording the results. I looked into each of those mirrors, and I'll tell you, you couldn't have destroyed those mirrors more completely if you'd taken a hammer to them."

"Wow," was all Gerardo could say.

"In the end, the joke was on him," I said. "He couldn't get any of the results on film because the lenses of the cameras blew up, too. I wasn't sad about it, though. In some weird way, it felt like I had won. It's like I had beaten science! Anyway, as we were leaving, I saw the professor guzzle a few swigs of whiskey from a flask, and I heard him say to his workers, 'That girl is so ugly, the mirrors don't just break, they break a sweat.'"

Gerardo laughed nervously, still not sure whether or not to entirely believe it.

So I leaned closer to him and whispered, "I'll show you if you want . . ."

He found me after the last bell had rung and the school was beginning to clear out. In his hand he had a little round makeup compact—the kind that flipped open with a mirror in the top half. He looked around at the crowds of kids going through their lockers and filtering out of school.

"Not here," he said. "Come on." He checked several classrooms, but they were either locked or there were teachers inside. Then he tugged on the door of the janitor's closet, and it swung wide. We checked to make sure no one was looking and stepped in, closing the door behind us. The room was cramped and smelled of Pine-Sol. I giggled. The janitor's closet was a notorious makeout spot. "Bet you never thought you'd be in the janitor's closet with me," I said.

"Don't gross me out," Gerardo answered. "So are you ready?"

"You may want to cover your eyes."

He didn't. Instead he held the little compact at arm's length and flipped it open. "Okay, what do I do now?"

"Just angle it toward me so I can see it."

He shifted it until I caught my reflection. The compact hummed for a second, like a cell phone set on vibrate, and the glass fractured into a hundred pieces. Some pieces stayed in the little round frame, some flew out. I felt a piece hit my blouse, then I heard it tinkle to the ground.

Gerardo just stared at the compact still clutched in his hand. "That," he said, "was the coolest thing I've ever seen."

Then he tilted his hand slightly. A piece of glass was sticking out of his wrist.

"Oh, crap!" He dropped the compact and reached for the glass with his other hand, grimacing as he pulled it out. It hadn't hit a major vein or anything. Just a couple of drops of blood spilled out. He put his wrist to his mouth to suck the blood off. When he looked at it again, it had already stopped bleeding. He looked at the half-inch sliver of glass in his other hand.

"You know what?" he said. "I'm going to keep this."

"What for?"

"Evidence," he said. "Evidence that Cara DeFido's got some kind of magic."

"Yeah, ugly magic," I said.

"That's better than no magic at all." Then he shook his head. "There's got to be some reason for it," he said.

Find the answers, I thought, and gently touched the pocket where the folded letter rested—but I kept the thought to myself.

That was the day I started wondering if maybe Gerardo was one of the answers I was supposed to find.

It wasn't just Nikki's compact mirror that broke that day. A barrier inside of me had broken as well—and Gerardo deciding to keep that little piece of glass made it even worse. I was feeling an emotion I had never allowed myself to feel for anyone. It was dangerous. The thing is, Gerardo acted *real* with me. He would act one way with his friends, another way with Nikki. But he didn't need to put up a front with me, because I was nothing to him. I guess, strangely, being nothing made me all the more important—and although he began as nothing to me, too—just another short-time occupant of the mercy seat—that was changing. Sure, he only sat with me once or twice a week, but on those days that he didn't, I began to feel a longing that would follow me through the rest of the day. All these years I'd kept my feelings for others covered as completely as the mirror in my room, but now that was changing.

Part of me knew those feelings would eventually choke me. But when something takes root, you can't stop its growth. It wasn't any old thing that was growing, either. My feelings for Gerardo were just like Miss Leticia's corpse flower: all ripe and ready to blossom into something that Gerardo would surely find repulsive.

8

INTO UGLY

The letter was just about burning a hole in my pocket. I could feel it there every minute of every day. Sometimes I could swear it was moving, rubbing itself against my leg to remind me it was there. Whenever Marisol walked by, giving me a sneer, instead of sneering back, I just reached into my pocket and brushed my fingertips across the smooth, soft paper. *You have a destiny,* that paper said. *Marisol can torture you all she wants, however she wants. No amount of roadkill will ever take that away.*

I stopped by the library after school one day, to do some investigating. I got on the Internet and searched for a town called De León. I found six of them, but all in different states, none in ours. So then I opened up the atlas—you know the one—it's so big that the library's got to have its own special stand for it. I searched every inch of our state on the map. No De León.

It had been two weeks since I got the letter, and I was still no closer to figuring out who had sent it or why.

I tried not to think too much about it, but the questions in my head just kept coming. How could somebody in some far-off place know what I needed to find? Have they been watching me? Should I be frightened? And what if, after all my searching, this was just another one of Marisol's stupid tricks, designed just to drive me crazy?

I pulled out the note and looked at it again. No. Marisol did not have a sweeping handwriting like this. Her letters were all happy and round. She dotted her *i*'s with hearts. And the paper— this wasn't the kind of paper you found in any stationery store. There was true magic in this note—I knew it in my heart, even if I didn't have any evidence. Yet.

"Can I help you?" the librarian asked.

"Huh?"

"You seem a bit confused; I was wondering if I could help you."

I looked around and found that I was standing in the quiet reading room, facing a blank wall. I hadn't even remembered walking there. I must have been wandering while looking at the note. It was just like the way I would wake up and find myself standing in the corner of my room. I had gotten used to that particular weirdness, but this was the first time I ever remembered wake-walking. I felt strangely unsettled and couldn't look that librarian in the eye.

"I'm fine," I told her.

She left, not all that sure that I was.

I'm so stupid—it's just three words, I told myself. Why should three words have such control over me? It was like some sort of magic spell.

Then I got to thinking about what Miss Leticia had said about words, letters having a magic to them when they were in the right order. Spells and spelling are one in the same. Spelling. Letters. The idea struck me at dinner one night so suddenly, I dropped my spoon right into my soup, and it splashed across the table, right into Vance's eye.

"Hey!"

"Excuse me." I got up, dinner suddenly forgotten, and went to my room, locking my door. My parents didn't question it, since I did it so often. Maybe they were glad to have me gone from the table. It was breakfast that Mom was determined to make a family meal. By the time dinner rolled around, she was too tired to care.

The second my door was locked, I went to my desk, pulled the note out of my pocket, and set it on my desk. Then I took out a piece of paper, my brush and ink. I let the tip of the brush soak in the silky blackness, then I closed my eyes, trying to feel a connection to the words. From my mind to my hand, to my fingers, to the tip of the brush. Then I opened my eyes and wrote in smooth simple strokes:

FIND THE ANSWERS

Even before I took the next step, I could sense I was onto something. It wasn't just the words, it was the letters. The letters and the spaces between. It was the spelling. It was the *spell*. I took the letters and began writing them down in different combinations.

FIND THE ANSWERS
DITHERS IN WRENF
STAINED WN FRESH

TRAIN WEDNES SHF
RAINS WHEN FEETS
THERE WINS FANDS
WHERE FINS STAND

That gave me a moment's pause. "Where Fins Stand." It didn't make any sense, yet somehow it sounded familiar. I searched my mind for the meaning, but I couldn't grab anything from those words. Still, there was some connection.

FIND THE ANSWERS . . . WHERE FINS STAND . . .

I shook my head to shake the thought loose and kept on playing with the letters, but no other combinations stood out in my mind. Eventually, I had to face the fact that I was on a wild-goose chase. As sure as I was that there was something hidden in those letters, logic told me to forget it. I closed the ink and crumpled the paper.

As for what happened next, well, I should have been smart enough to see it coming—or at least to step out of the way before I was hit. But I was so obsessed with figuring out the note, I never saw all the forces around me coming together. It wasn't so much a conspiracy of things as it was separate events weaving themselves together into a net that snared me sure as an animal trap.

The next day was a bad one. For one, all that time I'd been spending obsessing over the note kept me from studying, so I failed a math test. Then at lunch Gerardo spent the whole time talking about Nikki, and how good things were between the two of them. Well, they say bad news comes in threes—and when I got home on that day, I found my dad sitting on the sofa, across from none other than bad news number three: Marshall Astor, Marisol's boyfriend and accomplice in crime. My heart took a long, slow fall into my gut.

"What's he doing here?"

"Cara, honey," Dad said, standing up, "that's no way to talk to a guest."

"That's no guest, that's vermin. I'll get the rat poison."

Dad laughed nervously. "She's got a biting sense of humor, doesn't she? You two talk. I got some, um, business I have to take care of." Dad was out of that house at light speed.

I looked around, hoping Momma and Vance were there. Anything to keep me from being alone with Marshall, but they were nowhere to be found.

"So what do you want?" I asked. His foot was no longer bandaged, though he did still walk with a little bit of a limp. "If you want me to testify against Leticia Radcliffe, forget it."

"What? Oh. No, I never told nobody about that." I saw his toes wiggle in the tip of his shoes. He grimaced, and that just made me smile. I didn't usually enjoy other people's pain, but for Marshall Astor, I'd make an exception.

"Ruined your football season, I'll bet."

He shrugged. "I couldn't play anyway. I was already on academic probation."

I crossed my arms, making it clear I was done with the small talk. "So what do you want?"

"There's no point in beating around the bush," he said. "I'll just say it straight out. I'm asking you to the homecoming dance."

It caught me so off guard I just laughed out loud.

"I'm not making a joke," he said. "I'm serious."

"You think I'm gonna fall for that? What are you gonna do, wait till I get all dressed up and pour a bucket of blood on me? Sorry, I saw that movie."

"Nah, that's gross," he said. "I wouldn't do that."

"Oh, but it's not too gross to fill someone's room with roadkill?"

"I had nothing to do with that!" he said. Then he hesitated. "Well, okay, I did help Marisol scoop up the roadkill, but I didn't know what she was going to use it for."

I just looked at him in disbelief.

"I didn't!" he said. "I thought she had got it into her head that they needed a decent burial, or something. I didn't know she was gonna do what she did! I didn't find out until after."

I wasn't sure who was more of a fool—him for saying something like that, or me for actually believing him.

"So you're telling me Marisol has nothing to do with you asking me to the dance?"

"No," he said, "it's not Marisol's idea at all. In fact, she's pretty mad about it."

"Is that so?" Anything that made Marisol mad was fine by me—but I wasn't foolish enough to think Marshall was doing this out of the kindness of his microscopic heart.

"If it's not a Marisol scheme, then you must be doing it on a dare."

He shook his head. "You're so sure you're completely un-datable—well, maybe you're not. Maybe there are some decent things about the way you look."

"Name one."

He panicked for a moment, looking me up and down, trying to find something. Finally, he said, "You . . . uh . . . you've got nice hands."

Hah! Even if it were true, it wouldn't have made me believe his intentions. "I see right through you!" I told him. "You've got some secret reason for wanting to take me, and I want to know what it is!"

Suddenly he got all mad. He picked up a pillow and he threw it down hard. "Why do you gotta ask? Can't you just accept the invitation and leave it at that?"

Then I thought of Gerardo. I never even went so far as to imagine him inviting me to the dance, because I knew he was going with Nikki Smith. I tried to imagine myself with Marshall Astor, and I simply couldn't. "Who says I even want to go with you?"

He laughed—as if any girl in the world would be a fool to turn down an invitation from him. "You know what they say, Cara. Don't look a gift horse in the mouth." I thought he might make some crack about me looking like the gift horse, but he didn't.

"I only promise you two things," Marshall said. "One: This is not a trick. No one's gonna do anything bad to you, or they will answer to me. And two: You will have a good time."

"And how can you be so sure of that?"

Marshall smiled his winning smile. "Because if there's one thing I know, it's how to show a girl a good time."

And then he strutted out like so much peacock.

After he left, I stormed into my room, slamming the door, even though no one was there to hear it. I just liked the sound of hearing it slam. *Nice hands,* he had said. That was the best thing he could say about me, and even that was a lie. I was a nail-biter. More than that, I bit the skin around my nails, so both my hands always looked like a war zone.

But then I looked at my hands, and I realized that maybe Marshall was a bit more observant than me . . . because my fingertips weren't gnawed on at all. My nails were smooth, my cuticles were smooth. It looked as if I had just had a hundred-dollar manicure. It was impossible, because I'd been biting my nails more than ever. And yet they were perfect.

Like magic.

I gasped, and reached into my pocket, pulling out the shimmering note. I had been running my fingertips over its soft texture day after day, and my fingers had been healed. Repaired. Beautified. It was definitely a hint of something magical and mystical, but how far it went—how *deep* it went, was still a mystery.

"I'm not going."

"What do you mean you're not going?"

My momma was practically on her hands and knees, begging. "He is the handsomest boy in your grade, and if he's taken a liking to you—"

"He hasn't taken a liking to me," I told her. "Face it; there's something else going on here."

She put her hands on her hips. "Well, how do you know he isn't into ugly girls?"

The very concept completely derailed my train of thought.

"In this world," my momma said, "there is a man for every woman. You go to the mall, you look at people. Half the time they look so mismatched you wonder what's going on. But to them, they fit perfectly."

Vance sat in the recliner just enjoying the whole thing. Dad was in the kitchen, pretending not to listen, but I know he was.

"What are you gonna do for the rest of your life, Cara?" Momma asked. "You gonna lock yourself in your room? You gonna climb out that window and go walk around the cemetery your whole life?"

I snapped my eyes to her.

"You think I don't know you do that? I know every time you climb out that window, but I never say anything because I figure you've got a right to do the things you do."

"Fine. And I have a right not to go with Marshall anywhere," I said, but my resolve was failing. Then I got to thinking, if this whole thing wasn't some scheme of Marisol's, and if she truly didn't want Marshall to take me, then how could I pass up this chance to make her miserable? I thought about Gerardo, too. He'd be there with Nikki. Certainly, she wouldn't stand for him dancing with most other girls, but what about me? If Gerardo danced with me, would Nikki see that as him being noble? I could swallow my pride and pretend to be some social charity case if it meant Gerardo would dance with me. Then again, would he even ask? I'd never know if I stayed home.

I think Momma knew I was on the verge of giving in, because she got quiet. Serious.

"Honey, life does not throw you many opportunities," Momma said. "Don't go and squander the ones you get."

"But I don't like Marshall Astor."

"You don't have to," Momma told me.

And the look in her eyes when she said it struck home, because I knew she wasn't talking about me and Marshall. She was talking about her and Dad.

There were good things I could say about my momma and bad things. But the sadness I saw in her right then made me feel selfish thinking about myself.

"Go and be happy, Cara," Momma said. "I need you to be happy."

That fence I was sitting on had become too uncomfortable, so I finally jumped off. "Okay," I said. "I'll go."

I didn't tell Gerardo. I had planned to, but then he started talking all about how he and Nikki were going to the dance, and he asked me what I thought he should wear. After that, I didn't want to talk about it. No matter what awful fate awaited me at that party, it would be worth it to see the look on Gerardo's face when I walked in with Marshall!

9
▲
B-E-T-R-A-Y-A-L-S

The day before homecoming, Nikki went to get her teeth cleaned, determined that if she couldn't outshine the likes of Marisol and her beauty-queen friends, she could at least outsmile them. While Nikki's motormouth was being worked over, Gerardo had the afternoon free. So I took him to Vista View to meet Miss Leticia.

"This here's a good girl," Miss Leticia told him. "You treat her right, you hear?"

Gerardo put up his hands. "Hey, I'm not gonna treat her at all."

"Well," said Miss Leticia, "that's fine, too."

Miss Leticia seemed worried about something today. She wasn't saying anything, but it was right there in her body language.

"Are you okay?" I asked her.

"Oh, I'm fine. I got my son and that wife o' his comin' over tomorrow, and they always set me on edge."

I didn't ask any more questions. Miss Leticia had told me how, every time they come over, they bring brochures from nursing homes—not good ones, but the cheap ones that give you a room, a bed, and, if you're lucky, something edible once in a while. The kind of place you wouldn't wish on your worst enemy. Okay, maybe your *worst* enemy, but no one else.

"Maybe the corpse flower will bloom and chase them away," I suggested.

She laughed at that. "Maybe so, maybe so. It sure is gettin' ready."

"The *what* flower?" asked Gerardo.

"Come on, I'll show you."

Miss Leticia went inside, leaving us to walk through the greenhouse. There was a sour smell in the air, like dirty socks, as we got close to the corpse flower. Its stalk was now almost six feet high. You could see the crack where the flower would start to unfurl. "When it blooms it smells like dead bodies," I told him.

"Cool," he said. "I hope she opens up the doors so the whole town gets a whiff. The ultimate stink bomb!"

I thought it would be perfect if we were holding hands as we walked among the plants, but I knew that wasn't going to happen. Still, I tried to keep my hands in full view, hoping he'd notice how nice they'd been looking. He didn't, but he did make another observation.

"You know, I don't know why they call you the Flock's Rest Monster," Gerardo said. "There's nothing monstrous about you. Except maybe for the way you look, but looks don't make a monster. It's the things a person does."

"I don't know," I told him. "I've done some pretty monstrous things."

"Tell me one."

And so I told him all about how I got Marisol expelled from school.

"Hmm," said Gerardo when I was done. "Well, you didn't do anything monstrous at all. Marisol brought that on herself."

"So what about you?" I asked him. "What bad things have you done?"

He looked away from me then, tugged off a loose fern leaf, and fiddled with it.

"I've done some stuff."

"Tell me."

He kept his eyes on the fern in his hands instead of me.

I could tell there was something he wanted to say, yet didn't want to say at the same time. I wondered which part of him would win out.

"Go on, it's okay," I told him.

"No, it's not," he said. "But I'll tell you anyway." He took a deep breath. "You know, I almost got expelled, too. It was last year. They weren't just going to expel me, they were going to send me to juvie."

"I didn't know that." And then I asked as gently as I could, "What did you do?"

"I hacked into the district's computer. I didn't change grades or anything. I just got onto the teachers' Web sites and had some fun. I put pictures of monkeys in place of their faces, stuff like that."

I grinned. "I didn't know you were a computer geek."

He shrugged. "I'm not. It's just a hobby, you know."

"Well, that's not so bad," I told him.

"Yeah." Then he paused. "I swore I'd never do anything like

that again. But about a month ago, your friend Marisol asked me to hack into another computer."

"Marisol wanted you to fix up her grades?"

He shook his head. "No. She wanted me to do something else."

I still didn't get where this was going. Usually, I'm quicker, but not this time. I just stood there cluelessly waiting to hear what despicable thing Marisol had asked him to do.

"Anyway, she pulled out a stack of bills from her purse. I don't know where she got it from. I tell her no, but she keeps peeling off twenties . . . until I finally say yes."

"So what did she ask you to do?"

He looked at me like I should already know . . . but when I looked back at him, still clueless, he finally said: "She had me hack into a certain computer, and put in a secret wireless Web connection, so I could control the computer from my laptop . . . and choose the words it was asking people to spell . . ."

It was like getting hit broadside by a truck. You don't see it coming, and by the time you hear the crunch, it's too late.

We sat there for a long time, the sour-sock smell from the corpse plant getting stronger and stronger. We couldn't look at each other. The silence was so loud, if someone didn't break it, I felt I'd go deaf. Well, if he wouldn't do it, then I would.

"Don't sit by me in the lunchroom anymore," I told him.

"Yeah. Yeah, right," he said, then he set his hands in his pockets and walked away.

I felt the breeze as he opened the greenhouse door, then I heard him say, "For what it's worth, those words I made you spell . . . I don't think any of those words apply to you." Then I heard the door close, leaving me in a cell of captured beauty about to be overwhelmed by the smell of death.

I started walking home, my mind a storm of bad feelings and bad thoughts. Normally, I would have been able to stand up to this the way I stood up to most everything. I was good at not letting myself get hurt anymore. But this time I'd been careless. I'd become vulnerable, and Gerardo's betrayal, well, it hurt like a wound so deep it scraped bone.

I don't know if you would call what I had a blind fury, but whatever it was, I lost track of where I was, and where I was going. Eventually, I got my feelings under control by thinking of my calming place. The lush valley, the pastel-colored cottages. The sense of belonging. I let it flow over me like a trance as I walked. When I came out of it, it was like waking up after sleepwalking. It took me a few seconds to get my bearings.

I had set out toward home, but somewhere along the way, I had changed directions. Now I was near the edge of the town, close to the interstate. I was just standing in an empty lot, facing the mountains.

What's more is that I felt an urge to keep on going, like a kind of gravity pulling me in a direction other than down. I stood there for the longest time, trying to understand that feeling. But the afternoon was wearing on. The sun was about to set, and I was feeling cold in a place deep inside. Finally, I gave up and turned around to head home—but not before I realized the direction I was facing. Northwest.

———

If I was gonna find the answers, I knew I wouldn't find them at the homecoming dance. Still, I went out with Momma to get a gown, and then I prepared for the first date of my life.

I sat in my room, in front of the sheet-covered mirror, wondering what I looked like, playing the game again, reaching up to tear down the sheet, only to pull my hand back like a coward.

"You look positively"—Momma grappled for the word—"fetching," she said.

Vance peeked in and laughed. "Yeah, as in 'Here, Rover, go fetch!'"

I threw a curler at him.

"You don't listen to him," Momma said. She kissed me and did what last-minute triage she could on my hopeless hair.

The doorbell rang, and Dad answered it. It was Marshall, all dressed up in a suit he had already grown out of. He didn't look all too happy, but he didn't look all that miserable, either.

He shook my dad's hand.

"You make sure my daughter has a good time tonight," he said, with a sternness in his voice I rarely heard.

"Yes, sir," said Marshall.

He looked at me. I was afraid he was going to burst out laughing. But instead he said, "That's a pretty dress you got on, Cara."

Momma nudged my shoulder. "Thank the boy, dear."

"Thanks," I said.

As much as I hated to admit it, I was a little bit excited—and fearful, too—but I was walking into this with my eyes open. If Marisol, Marshall, or whoever had something awful planned for me, they would not get the satisfaction, because whatever it was, I would throw it back in their faces.

Out front, Marshall had himself a car. Nothing fancy, mind you. Just an old Chevy that had passed hands maybe two or three times before landing with him.

"Nice make-out car," I said to Marshall with a smirk. "Don't get any ideas. I'm not that kind of girl."

He rolled his eyes. "Don't worry. You're safe."

"Am I?" I said. "How about when we get there? How safe will I be then?"

He started the car and laughed. "You still think we're pulling some prank on you, huh? I told you, it's nothing like that."

"So then what's tonight about?" I asked.

"It's about going to a dance, having a good time, and taking you home. And then driving away."

"And then what?"

A frightened expression came over his face. "What do you mean, 'then what?'"

"What happens then? You gonna take me to other parties? Or is this like the lottery, one date with Marshall Astor."

He thought for a moment and then said, "Just enjoy tonight. We'll let tomorrow take care of itself."

When we got there, the party was in full swing. Couples dancing. The shy ones standing on the sidelines.

It wasn't until I saw Marisol that I knew Marshall had been telling the truth. That bitter-sour look on her face when she saw us made it clear to me she'd had no part in this, and wanted no part of it, either. For the rest of the night, she tried to avoid us and busied herself with her friends and dancing with dateless boys. I, of course, did everything I could to be in her line of sight as often as possible. I even made a point of running into her in the bathroom.

"Isn't this one of the signs that the world is about to end?" I said to her.

"Excuse me?"

"You know—hell freezes over, rivers turn to blood, and Marisol doesn't have a date?"

She bristled like a porcupine, then tossed it off with a flick of her perfect hair. "Poor Marshall," she said. "After tonight, I'll need to disinfect him." Then she strutted out—but stumbled clumsily on her high heels, clinching this as the high point of my evening.

Marshall, to my amazement, was a perfect gentleman. He danced with nobody but me all night! Even the slow dances, with his hands around my waist.

First it felt so strange, so awkward. I had never been that close to a boy. Every time we took a break from dancing, he got me some punch. He treated me with the respect I didn't think he could give anyone, and I dared to start thinking that maybe I had misjudged him. Maybe, as bad as he was, there was a good side trying to come through.

Don't you believe it, Cara, a voice in my head told me, but I was starting to enjoy myself too much to pay it any mind.

It could have been the perfect evening—in fact, it would have been, if it hadn't been for one thing.

Gerardo Sanchez.

An hour into the party, Gerardo arrived with Nikki Smith clinging to him like kudzu, and he was clinging right back. They were a couple, I knew that in theory—but actually seeing it with my own eyes was too much to take. It set my blood on a long, slow boil, and not even the sight of Marisol on the sidelines without a dance partner could make me feel better.

Each time Marshall and I danced, they were both there dancing, too.

I caught Gerardo's eye, but he didn't acknowledge me. Maybe he was too ashamed or embarrassed by his confession. Maybe he was just freaked that I was there with Marshall.

The thing is, even though I had the best-looking boy in front of me, teaching me dance moves, getting me punch, treating me like I wasn't the Flock's Rest Monster, I knew he wasn't the one I wanted. No matter what Gerardo had done that day at the spelling bee, it was him that I wanted to be holding me in those slow dances, with those clumsy hands and those skinny arms.

But those skinny arms were wrapped around Nikki, and I began to hate her like I hated Marisol.

The boiling in my blood started making its way to my brain, and I started doing some crazy things.

I watched Gerardo and Nikki dance, so I danced harder with Marshall. I watched how close they danced in the slow numbers, and I pulled Marshall that close to me whether he liked it or not.

"Uh, Cara, I think we should sit this one out," Marshall said.

"No," I told him. "You said we're gonna have a good time, and I say I want to dance."

I half expected him to storm away, but he didn't.

Then, as the night got later, and all the dances started to become slow, the jealous vein throbbing through my body just hemorrhaged, until it was all I could feel.

And that's when I saw it.

I saw Gerardo look into Nikki's eyes, and pull her into that perfect embrace in the middle of a slow song. They kissed, and kissed, and didn't stop.

I looked to Marshall. He looked at me with some kind of terror in his eyes, but I didn't care. I grabbed him by the tie, pulled him toward me, and planted a kiss on him, the likes of which he will never forget.

With all of his jock strength, he could not pull away. I had him locked in that kiss like a boot on a car tire—and the couples around us pulled back until we were there, standing by ourselves. His arms, which had at first been struggling, were now limp, weak, like a rag doll.

That'll show him, I said to myself. *That'll show Gerardo. He can have Nikki, but look at me. I've got Marshall Astor!*

Finally, I let Marshall go, and he stepped away, catching his breath. His mouth opened and closed a few times, like a fish that had flipped out of its bowl.

"Uuugggghhhh!"

He brought the back of his hand up to his mouth, wiped his lips, and didn't stop there. He practically put his whole hand in his mouth, rubbing at his gums and teeth, as if he could just pull the kiss out. And when he realized that the kiss just wasn't going away, he started to go a little bit pale.

"Forget this," he said. His eyes were locked on me, and the expression of horror and helplessness on his face made me, for the first time, truly feel like the monster they said I was.

He reached into his pocket, pulled out his car keys, and hurled them at me. They hit my dress and jangled to the ground.

"Nothing is worth this," he said. "Tell your father he can keep his car! I don't want it!" His face started to pass through several shades of green. His cheeks swelled.

Then he turned, looking for the nearest trash can, but the closest thing he found was, unfortunately, the punch bowl.

I didn't think he would do it, but that kiss must have been so disgusting to him, nothing could stop nature now. And before the whole school, Marshall Astor threw up into the homecoming punch bowl.

10

▲

TEMPEST
AND A TEAPOT

I tore out of the party faster than Cinderella at midnight, and I left no shoe behind. I didn't leave those car keys behind, either; I picked them up before I headed out. The jealousy I felt just moments before had played itself out, and all that remained was humiliation. This time those kids in there hadn't played a trick on me—I had played the trick on myself

I didn't know who to be more horrified by: myself for what I had done; Marshall, for finding me so utterly repulsive; or my father, who, in his misguided desire to see me happy, had offered Marshall Astor a used car from his lot in return for taking me to the homecoming dance.

Is that the going rate for spending time with me? I thought. *A Chevy for your troubles?*

Well, I had the keys to that car now. The lot was speckled with rain, and a chill in the wind made it clear that these were the first drops of a storm. *Let it rain,* I thought. *Let their tailored suits and chiffon dresses get drenched and ruined. Let lightning strike and take down the power, so there'll be no more slow dancing for anyone.*

I got behind the wheel and peeled out of that parking lot before anyone could come out and stop me. When Momma had taught me to drive, she angled the mirrors away from me. But these weren't. I caught my eyes in the rearview mirror. It shattered. Little bits of glass were next to me on the front seat, and I thought of the sliver of glass Gerardo had kept. Did it mean anything at all to him? Did he think of it once while he was in there with his lips firmly pressed against Nikki Smith's freshly cleaned teeth like a sucker fish? The fact that I even cared just made me feel worse.

I knew I couldn't go home. I couldn't face my parents now, especially my father, knowing the part he had played in this. There was only one person to talk to now. The woman whose clouded eyes couldn't see me.

It started to rain heavier, and the windshield wipers pounded out a drumbeat, primal and ominous. Now the tears I'd been holding back—not just today, but all my life—burst from my eyes, so that I could barely see. The tears were full of all the things I could never be. All the dreams denied me because of a face too hideous to see its own reflection.

The sobs came with such strength, I couldn't catch my breath. The tears blurred my vision even more than the rain. I never even saw the gate of Vista View Cemetery until I plowed through it, crashing it open. I flew around the curves of the road winding up the hill and skidded to a halt at the top, right in front of Miss Leticia's house. A white van and an expensive car were in the driveway. I didn't stop to think what they might be doing there. Instead I ran to the front door and pounded and pounded and pounded until she finally answered.

"Cara? What are you doing here? You shouldn't be here,

honey, this ain't a good time at all." She looked careworn in a way I'd never seen before.

"Please, Miss Leticia—let me come in! I have to talk to you, I just have to!"

She looked past me, into the rain. "You here alone?"

"Yes."

She sighed. "All right, then. Come on in—but only for a bit."

She led me quickly past the darkened living room and into the kitchen. "Whose cars are out front?" I asked. "Do you have guests?"

"Yes," she said. "Guests." She pulled out a chair from the kitchen table and practically forced me down into it. "You sit right here, and I'll be back in a minute. Don't you move from that spot!"

"I won't."

I was so relieved to be there, out of the rain, away from my life, it didn't hit me how odd she was acting. I was cold and her house was warm, that's all I cared about right then. Then I saw something else that could warm me up. Miss Leticia's tea tray was right there on the kitchen table. I poured myself a cup. The tea was light-colored—not like the tea she usually made. When I picked up the cup, there was no steam coming from it. It was cold. Well, I thought, her tea was something special, hot or cold. I brought it up and smelled it, trying to identify what kind it was. It had a grassy, bitter smell.

Suddenly I heard a scream, and I looked up to see Miss Leticia racing toward me. She swung her hand and sent that teacup flying across the room, and it smashed against the wall. I stared at her in shock.

"That tea is not for you!" she said. "Did you drink any?"

"No," I said weakly. I was confused and more than a little bit frightened now.

"That's good, then. That's good." She relaxed. That's when I noticed she had a little wicker suitcase. It had been packed so hastily, the sleeve of a flowery blouse was sticking out of the side. "Maybe you just better go. I know you got troubles, but so do I. Now's just not a talkin' time."

My brain, which had been in power-saver mode since I got there, finally kicked in. It wasn't so much the suitcase or even the quivering tone of her voice that clued me in. It was the look on her empty-eyed face. That look spelled a hundred things, none of them good.

"Miss Leticia," I asked slowly, "what happened here?"

She clamped her hand over her mouth as if to hold back a wail, then took a deep breath. "That van is from the hospital. The car belongs to a doctor. I can't recall his name."

"Hospital?" I said. "Are you sick?"

"Not that kind of hospital."

It took a moment, but then I understood. Even before she said it, I knew why they were here.

"My son and that awful wife of his—they signed papers, and had me committed. Didn't even have the decency to come themselves—they sent the doctor to come here and take me away." She gripped her arms, obviously cold like me, even in the heat of the room. "Old age does terrible things to you . . . but the things we do to each other are worse."

I stood up and looked out the kitchen door toward the dark living room. The truth was dawning on me much faster than I wanted it to. It wasn't just *my* life that had fallen apart tonight.

Wise and wonderful Miss Leticia Radcliffe suddenly wasn't so wise, and wasn't so wonderful. I took a step forward.

"Don't you go in there!" she shouted.

For a brief instant a lightning flash lit up the living room. I saw a hand hanging over the arm of a high-backed chair. The hand wasn't moving.

"Miss Leticia . . . what did you do?"

And helplessly she said, "I made them some tea."

Thunder rolled like the breath of a beast and echoed back from the mountains.

"It was only supposed to put them to sleep, so I would have time to get away," she said. "But I used too much lily of the valley! I made it too strong."

I stood there, unable to say anything, because my insides had started a war.

See, there's a part of you that's an enemy of the mind. It's the heart of inspiration and imagination . . . but it's also the heart of terror and paranoia. That part of me welled up at that awful moment and said to me, *This is your fault. You cursed this poor old woman, just like you cursed your family. Your ugliness touched her and grew into* this *ugliness.* No amount of sensible, rational thought was going to make that voice go away.

"Where will you go?"

"I got old friends in old places," she said. "I can still catch the late bus if I leave now."

"I'll drive you!"

"No!" she said, her voice like the thunder itself. "That would be aiding and abetting, and I will *not* bring you into this." Then her voice became quiet again. "I know where the Greyhounds stop, and I can see well enough to get there. You best leave here," she told me. "Go home."

"I can't go home."

"Then go someplace else. I'm sorry, Cara, I can't help you anymore." Then she picked up her little suitcase and left.

I stood there in the middle of her kitchen, unable to do anything but listen to the rain pounding on the windows like it was the start of the great flood. And then something occurred to me. Something awful.

"Miss Leticia! Wait!"

I raced to the door, not daring to look toward the living room. I burst out into the rain and looked around. It was dark, but I could make her out. She was waddling her way across the hill, taking a shortcut to the main road.

Got a grandson calls me Nana Cyborg, she had said, *on accounta all this metal.*

She was a single figure in the open grass, while up above the sparking clouds roiled like it was Armageddon.

"Miss Leticia! Stop!"

I raced out to the waterlogged hill. She didn't stop, she didn't turn.

"Come back!"

And then the heavens exploded. All I saw was a blinding white flash. I felt the thunder more than heard it, and the electric charge knocked me off my feet. It sizzled through me like scarabs beneath my skin, and then it was gone. I knew I had felt only a hint of the lightning. The inky darkness returned, and the stench of ozone filled the air. I ran to Miss Leticia. The grass around her was singed and smoking, even in the rain. She was sprawled on the ground, trembling. Her dress was smoldering like the grass.

"C . . . C . . . Cara."

"We've got to get you inside!"

I looked around. The nearest structure was the greenhouse, its back entrance just about fifty yards away. I tried to lift her, but she was too heavy. In the end, I had to drag her across the hill by her armpits. I pulled open the door of the greenhouse, and was laid low by a stench more awful than anything I could remember. Miss Leticia groaned, then grinned. I pulled her over the threshold, and we collapsed in a bed of begonias.

That smell—it was like the horrible stench of meat left to rot in the hot, hot sun. A smell like my roadkill room, only ten times worse, and there were flies everywhere.

"It bloomed," Miss Leticia said weakly. "It finally bloomed."

There, just a few feet away from us, I could see the corpse flower's huge bloom. It had the shape of a teacup, but three feet wide and four feet high, surrounding that six-foot stalk.

Flies buzzed over the brim, in and out, in and out, pollinating the hideous thing.

Now it was complete. Now everything in the world had gone rancid.

"Isn't it wonderful?" she said.

"We've got to get you help."

"No help. No help. Already got my wish," she said. Her arm fluttered slightly. I took her hand. "The good Lord saw fit to keep me where I want to be. I got a plot waiting on the south side of the hill. It's good there. It's good."

I wanted to tell her to hold on. I wanted to tell her she'd

come through, but it would have been a lie. "Please don't go," I begged, even though I knew I was being selfish. Because I needed her. She must have known what I was thinking, because tears came to her clouded eyes. "I'm sorry," she said. "I promised I would be here to see your destiny." She gripped my hand with the last of her strength. "Go find it," she said. "You go find the answers."

She didn't go limp. She didn't even loosen her grip. But in a moment her eyes, as lifeless as they had seemed before, became truly glazed with the emptiness of death, and I knew she was gone. I rolled her gently onto her back, closed her eyelids, and folded her hands over her chest. Then I tore two massive petals from her beloved corpse flower and covered her body.

I cried for her. They say when you cry for the dead, you're really crying for yourself, and maybe partly I was. My life had become one betrayal after another. Gerardo, Marshall, my parents. Now fate itself had stolen the only person in my life who hadn't betrayed me. I was alone now—really alone—and in that dark lonely moment, I dared to tempt fate. Not just tempt it, but challenge it.

The lights of the greenhouse were reflected in its many windows. At night, in the rain, you couldn't see anything beyond the glass. I pushed aside the big rhododendron and fern leaves until I caught my own gaze in the glass: my rain-drenched hair, my sagging gown, my awful cheeks and chin and teeth, all reflected painfully back at me.

Then that glass did what nature told it to. It shattered—and not just the window in front of me: It began a chain reaction around the entire greenhouse. One pane after another crackled and blew out, until the air was white with falling crystal, jabbing the plants and ground, piercing my dress, my skin.

And I screamed, not out of physical pain, but a pain much deeper, and much greater.

When it was done, the greenhouse was nothing but a skeleton. All that remained was the iron frame and the shredded fragments of plants.

I could have crumbled, too. God knows I wanted to. Just fall into a heap until they found me there.

But it's in those moments when your world falls apart that you discover what you truly are made of. And I was not made of broken glass.

One by one, I pulled the shards from my arms and shoulders and scalp, dropping them on the ground. Then I walked out of that place, got into the Chevy my father had so unwittingly provided me, and left town.

11

▲

NORTHWEST

I had no money, I had no destination, but that didn't matter. When your only desire is to leave, any direction you take is the right one, as long as you don't turn around. I was still bleeding from the greenhouse glass, but I made myself believe it didn't matter. I would close the wounds with the sheer force of my will.

My life as I knew it was gone. It was now a blank page—that white void waiting to be carved into a new form by brush and ink. Who I would be was still a mystery, and in that car, in transit between a horrible past and an unknown future, I felt the terror and excitement of a babe at the moment of its birth.

A powerful sense of determination overtook me. Maybe it was just shock and loss of blood, or maybe it was something else. It felt magical—like a string was wrapped around my soul and pulling me forward, and if I didn't stomp on that accelerator, heading down those country roads to God knows where, that string would have pulled me right through the windshield to wherever it wanted me to go.

Like I said, any direction would have been fine, as long as it took me away from Flock's Rest—but I wasn't going in just any old direction, was I? I realized that pretty quick.

I was heading northwest. And this time, for the first time, I didn't resist the pull.

There were few cars out on a night like this, and with every mile I put between me and Flock's Rest, I began to feel my spirits lift.

Every few miles on that rain-drenched highway, I saw reminders of what I was leaving behind that made me kick up the rpm and push the Chevy harder. It was those signs by the side of the road, blooming in my headlights. Those old faded billboards advertising my father's cars.

Ten miles out, I saw my father's smiling face. The billboard read DEFIDO MOTORS: CLASSIC CARS FROM CLASSY TIMES.

Nineteen miles out, there he was again, the billboard showing him sitting on the roof of a used car, holding an American flag— as if buying used cars and patriotism were one and the same. DEFIDO MOTORS TRIED & TRUE.

Twenty-seven miles out, a billboard featuring my momma in her pink Cadillac, pointy tail fins and all. DEFIDO MOTORS, WHERE FINS STAND FOR STATUS.

I realized that the gravity was pulling me due west now. But there were no roads that went that way. Although I couldn't see them, I knew what was west of me. The mountains. The nearest road that crossed them was miles away.

I was approaching the county line. Just a few more of my father's old signs, and I'd be out of his sphere of influence for good. My gas tank was full. My mind was set. And nothing could stop me from escaping forever that hideous place "where fins stand for status."

Even in my weakened state, I couldn't help but get stuck on that phrase. It kept coming back to my mind. *DeFido Motors, Where Fins Stand for Status.*

Find the answers . . . Where . . . fins . . . stand . . .

I slammed on the brakes so hard I fishtailed, and did a full one-eighty. I found myself facing the wrong way in the lane, with a truck bearing down on me.

I hit the accelerator and pulled off the road, landing in a ditch. The truck barely missed me, its blaring horn changing pitch as it swerved past.

Now my wheels spun in mud, and I knew there was no getting this car out of the ditch. Dizziness almost overtook me then. I clutched the steering wheel and closed my eyes until the feeling passed.

Then I got out of the car and headed back to the billboard on foot.

It was about a mile back. In the darkness, it looked completely black. Only in flashes of lightning could I see it now, and only for a second. My momma looked so happy in the picture, but that was a long time ago. Now the old billboard was falling victim to the elements. Another year or so, and a few more storms like this, and it would be down completely. One side leaned forward, the other side leaned back, the wood was pulling apart, and the paint had faded and peeled.

Find the answers . . . where fins stand . . .

Right behind the billboard was a narrow, weed-choked path leading through dense trees and up a hill into darkness. I took the path and headed off toward the mountains.

The rain turned to sleet, and although the cold numbed the

pain of my wounds, it also stole what little body heat I had left. I couldn't feel my fingers, couldn't feel my toes, could barely feel pain when I tripped and smashed my knee against a stone. I wanted to sleep more than anything, but I knew if I did, I'd die. It would be years before they found my body out here, if they ever found it at all. Resting was out of the question. The only thing to do was push forward, following the path, following the gravity until I reached its center.

I stumbled up one hill and down another, over and over, each hill steeper than the one before.

I can't remember when I stopped walking. I don't remember falling down. But I do remember the feeling of cold mud against my back. I do remember the stinging feeling of sleet hitting my eyes as I lay on the ground, making it hard to see anything.

Now I can sleep, I thought. *Now I can sleep, and I'll be fine.*

And I do remember the angels looking down on me. Solemn faces and gray robes that must have been hiding their wings. They took me in their warm hands and lifted me up.

Finally, I closed my eyes, satisfied, because I knew they were taking me to my reward.

PART TWO

▲

"Eternessence"

12

a feast of flowers

You can't wake up and still think you're dead.

No matter how strange your surroundings, there's something about being made of flesh and bone that tells you instinctively you haven't left it all behind. And so, when I opened my eyes to see a room with bright white walls and no windows, I knew I wasn't in heaven—but I wasn't anyplace on earth I knew, either. The light came from a large skylight above me, and through it I could see a clear blue sky. The rainstorm had passed.

"Good morning!"

I didn't know anyone was beside me until I heard the voice. I turned to see him sitting there next to the bed. A boy. He wasn't much older than me. He was clean-cut, had blond hair, a clear complexion, and pastel blue eyes. When he smiled I thought I recognized him, but knew I was wrong. His smile held no hint of deception; it was an honest smile, and I knew no one like that.

I sat up, expecting to feel weak, but I didn't. I felt completely rested.

"Hi, I'm Aaron," he said, and gently took my hand.

His clothes were white, and at first I figured this to be a

hospital—but the style of his clothes was not hospital-like at all. He wore an eggshell-white shirt, and an eggshell white vest. Even his pants were that same soft shade of white. It was such an odd combination, and yet it seemed so perfect, you might wonder why everyone didn't dress like this.

Aaron was handsome. Truly so. Not in a Marshall Astor kind of way, but in a way that went beyond mere good looks. I was happy just to gaze at him, then I silently scolded myself for being so foolish. That's when I realized where I'd seen him before.

"I . . . I've been dreaming about you!"

He smiled gently, as if this were no surprise to him. "You probably have lots of questions," Aaron said.

I nodded.

"Well, come with me," he said. "Time to find the answers."

Like I said, I knew I was alive—no question about that, and yet when I stepped out of that little white room, I found myself in paradise. It wasn't just any paradise, either—it was *my* special one. "Nowhere Valley." This was the place I went when I closed my eyes. Oh, I didn't get it exactly right in my head; the mountains around this valley were higher than the ones in my mind. The houses I had always pictured in soft tones of blues and yellows were all eggshell white, and built in little clusters around the valley, not evenly spaced like I had imagined. But otherwise, it was every bit the same. The valley was the greenest I've ever seen, about a mile long. A stone path began at the small one-room cottage where I awoke and wound like a lazy river from this end of the valley to the other. If this was my new life, then everything I had been through had been worth it!

"Welcome to De León," said Aaron. Then he took my hand without any of the hesitation a boy usually has when taking the hand of a girl, and he led me down into the valley.

My body ached as I walked, but I was so focused on the sights it didn't matter. At the first house we passed, a couple in their twenties was sitting on a porch swing, sipping lemonade, and they waved to us. Their clothes were the same shade of white as Aaron's, which I now knew were soft as velvet, pure as satin. I looked down at what I was wearing. They had taken away my shredded gown and given me a white dress as well, but it wasn't made of the same material as their clothes. What I wore was cotton, but their clothes made the purest cotton look as ugly as a potato sack.

The couple came forward. "Good morning, Aaron," the man said. "Hello, Cara. It's good to have you here."

I looked at Aaron, gaping. "But . . . how does he know my name?"

"Shhh," Aaron said gently. "Just take it in. Enjoy it."

Then the couple clipped some flowers from their beautiful garden and threw them in the path in front of us. I tried to walk around them, but Aaron wouldn't let me. "No," he said. "Walk over them. Crush the petals beneath your feet so their fragrance fills the air."

And so I did.

At every house we passed, people stopped whatever they were doing to say hello, and to throw flowers in our path. One woman came running out of her house to give me a gentle hug. "I'm so glad you pulled through," she said. "My name is Harmony."

Harmony was beautiful—perhaps Momma's age, but without the world-weariness that weighed on my mother's face. In fact, everyone here was beautiful. It wasn't a plastic, fake beauty, like fashion models, or like Marisol. Nothing so skin-deep. Like my ugliness, their beauty went to the bone.

"I tended to your wounds, and Aaron and I took turns sitting with you," Harmony told me. I could still feel those wounds from the greenhouse glass, which had cut me in so many places. I looked at the long gash on my arm. There was no bandage, even though the wound was still red and a bit swollen. It had been stitched closed by sutures so fine I could barely see them. In fact, all my wounds had been sewed the same way.

"I did all the work," Harmony said proudly. "Ninety-five stitches in all."

"Harmony's our seamstress here," Aaron said.

The fact that I was sewn up by a seamstress didn't sit well with me. "No offense, but . . . aren't there any doctors here?"

Neither of them answered right away. Then Harmony said, "We get by without."

I wanted to ask how—or more importantly, *why*—but Aaron gently urged me forward along the path.

Along the way, more flowers were tossed at my feet by smiling residents of the valley, and the perfume of the crushed petals filled the air around me. I began to realize that this was part of some ritual. It made me think of a punishment I heard about from the olden days. When a soldier was found guilty of some criminal act, the other men formed two lines and the offender had to pass between them, while the other men beat him with their fists, or with sticks, or with whatever they wanted to use. It was called a *gauntlet,* and "running the gauntlet" left a man broken in more ways than one. Well, this was an anti-gauntlet, and the men and women on either side of the road delivered pleasure rather than pain, offering me good wishes and flowers before my feet. I had never felt so accepted in my life.

You might think such a thing would feel good, but you have to understand I wasn't used to acceptance. It felt strange. It was, in its own way, terrifying, and by the time I had come to the far end of the path, my hands and legs were shaking as if the men and women *had* beaten me.

Aaron put his hand around my waist to give me support as we passed the last of the homes, as if he understood exactly how I felt.

At the end of the path loomed a mansion—the last structure before the walls of the valley closed in. The double doors were wide open and inviting. I hesitated. Experience told me that sometimes the most inviting places are just to lure you to something awful. I tried to sense deceit or hidden intentions in Aaron. Either there were none, or my intuition was broken.

"Come on," Aaron said, gently easing me forward. "He's waiting for you."

"Who's waiting for me?"

Aaron smiled. "We just call him *Abuelo.*" Grandfather.

The mansion had dozens of rooms. Through the open doors I saw a library, a sunroom, and a huge kitchen. Music poured from the entrance of a grand salon, harpsichord and violin. There was joyous laughter everywhere, and then it occurred to me that with all the voices I heard, both in the valley and in here, I had not heard a single child. It seemed Aaron and I were the youngest ones here. With so many happy couples, shouldn't there be children? I thought to ask Aaron, but the thought was blasted out of my mind by the sight before me as we neared the center of the mansion.

There was a wide marble staircase, leading up to a closed mahogany door adorned in gold. This was the only door I had seen in the entire mansion that wasn't open.

Aaron stopped at the bottom of the stairs.

"Don't be afraid," Aaron said. "Go on. He's expecting you."

I could feel my heart pounding against my ribs, and I thought for sure it would burst halfway up, and I'd tumble back down the stairs. Still, I forced myself forward until I was at the top of the stairs, then I reached for the golden knob on the huge mahogany door and leaned against the door with all my weight.

The door slowly creaked open, and I slipped through the gap into a huge oval ballroom. There were no windows, only a skylight, just like in the tiny room where I had first woken up. The walls here, however, weren't white. They were painted black, and on every wall there were dozens of picture frames—rectangular, square, oval—and every single one of them was covered by the same soft white cloth everyone's clothes were made of. I wondered what artwork could be so precious that no one was allowed to see it.

"Finalmente!" said a voice both gentle and rough.

He sat on a soft padded settee at the far end of the room, in the shaft of light brought in by the skylight.

"Vengas aqui, mi hija." When I didn't move, he sighed, and resorted to English. "Come here, my child."

I approached across the black marble floor, cold beneath my bare feet.

The old man had a glow about him that had nothing to do with the light of the sun. It was an inner radiance. He was truly old—perhaps as old as poor Miss Leticia had been—but the vitality in his eyes was like that of a man in his twenties.

"Did you enjoy your *pascua de florida*? Your feast of flowers? I can still smell the blossoms on your feet."

"It was . . . uh . . . interesting."

"Forgive me," he said. "I am a man in love with ceremony."

Now that I was just a few feet away, I could see that his skin was marred by deep wrinkles, but that didn't lessen how handsome he was. Looking at his face was like looking at an ancient oak in the first days of summer—lined and wizened, and yet as gloriously green as a sapling.

But when he looked at me, clearly he saw something different. He saw my ugliness.

"Ah! That face, that face!" he said. "So many tears your face has drawn from you, *verdad?*"

"My face is my business," I told him.

"This is true. But you are here, so that makes it my business as well." Then he gestured all around him. "For you, I have covered all my mirrors."

So, it wasn't artwork on the walls around us.

He narrowed his keen eyes and took in the features of my face. "Hmm," he said. "*Qué feo.* What Aaron says is true. You are very, very ugly—but do not think you are special in this. You are not the first, you are not the last. And I have seen uglier."

If anyone else had said that, I would have called them a liar, but there was such authority in the old man's voice, everything he said rang true. There was a certain light to Abuelo, too. Not something I could see, but something I could *feel,* as irresistible as the pull of gravity, yet somehow a bit dangerous, like radiation. I'd call it *graviation. G-R-A-V-I-A-T-I-O-N.* Good word.

He smiled at me as if he could read my thoughts. If he told me he could, I would have believed him. I almost wanted him to, because it was so hard to put into words all the thoughts and feelings I had had since opening my eyes to this wonderful place.

"Why did you bring me here?" I asked.

He waved his hand. "I did nothing. You brought yourself here. Like a salmon swimming upstream, there was an instinct in you to find this place. My letter merely reminded you."

I gasped. "You wrote the letter!"

The old man smiled, showing teeth as pearly white as his suit. "I wrote it, yes. But it was Aaron who convinced me you were worth the effort."

"Aaron convinced you? But . . . I never met Aaron before."

The old man raised his eyebrows. "Well, Aaron knows of you, even if you do not know of him. And when you came through the mountains, it was he who was waiting with the monks for you."

"The monks?"

"Not your concern. They found you, freezing to death in the rain, and they brought you here. That's all you need to know."

I thought back to that rainy night. Was it yesterday? A week ago? How long had I been unconscious? "My parents are probably looking for me!"

"Let them look," Abuelo said. "They will not find you here. The earth itself conspires to keep this place hidden." Then he added, "Besides . . . do you truly believe they will search for long?"

I wanted to be furious at the question. I wanted to think my parents would tear the world apart trying to find me . . . but did I really believe that? My father, who secretly thought I was the curse that brought him a life of failure? My mother, to whom I'd been such a burden for all these years? How long would they try to find me? How much did they truly want to?

I turned my eyes down to the black marble floor. "I don't belong here," I told him. "I might not belong out there, but I *definitely* don't belong here."

"Perhaps this is true," the old man said, "but you are welcome to linger awhile. Who knows, in time, you may see things differently, *verdad?*"

I didn't think so, but whether I belonged here or not, I couldn't deny the sense of acceptance I felt. "Thank you," I said. I would stay, I decided. At least until the ugularity of my face sucked away their acceptance, and poisoned them against me, as I knew it eventually would.

13

▲

IT'S a BeaUTIFUL LIFe

I stayed in that little one-room cottage at the opposite end of the valley from Abuelo's mansion. When I had arrived, there was nothing in it but a bed, but each day someone else brought a single gift. The daily gifts were another one of Abuelo's rituals, I suppose. No one seemed to keep a calendar, so I marked the days by counting the things in my cottage. A table and chairs, a handblown glass oil lamp, a dresser.

Each morning I awoke to find Aaron sitting on my porch, waiting to take me to someone else's home for breakfast. I have to admit I liked that he was there, but all that attention from him made me self-conscious.

"Don't you have something better to do than babysit me?" I asked him on the third morning.

He shrugged. "There's plenty of time to do the things I've got to do," he said. "Besides, it's not babysitting."

I wondered whether it was his assigned chore to be my escort, or if he did it because he wanted to.

Time was spent differently here than in the outside world. Some people had generators to make electricity, but they rarely used them, which meant there were no televisions, or video games, or any of the usual things people use to occupy their time. You might think that would be horrible, but it wasn't. Or at least it wasn't in De León. People kept busy, each in their own way—and wherever I went, people invited me to be a part of whatever they were doing.

In Harmony's house, for instance, some of the women would get together and weave with her. She invited me in and taught me how to do it, creating that fine fabric for the clothes they wore. They sang while they wove, and taught me the songs so I could sing along. We worked the hand looms to the rhythm of the song. It wasn't exactly what you would call fun, but it was soothing, and satisfying in a way I can't explain. I sat there all day and hadn't realized that hours had passed until Harmony lit the lamps. I left that evening feeling like I'd accomplished something great.

I quickly learned that everyone had their place in De León—or I guess I should say everyone *made* their place. There were Claude and Willem—two craftsmen who carved furniture with so much love, you could just about feel their embrace when you sat in one of their rocking chairs. There was Haidy, who spent her days writing poetry, and her husband, Roland, who set it to music. Maxwell, the storyteller, would come to a different house each night and entertain better than the finest film, in return for being fed.

Even Aaron, the youngest of the men, at sixteen, had found his niche.

I asked him about it late one afternoon. We were sitting out by the small fishing pond, watching the early twilight sky change colors.

"What do you do all day?" I asked. "I mean, when you're not being my personal social director. Do you go to school? I don't see a little red schoolhouse anywhere in the valley."

"There is no school," he told me. "At least not the kind you're thinking about."

"Well then, this must be heaven after all."

"We learn from each other," he explained. "And what we can't teach, we can read up on in Abuelo's library. Abuelo even gives lectures on everything from philosophy to physics—whatever his current interest is."

"I guess when you've been around as long as he has, you become an expert in just about everything," I said. "But you still haven't answered my question. How do you fit in here?"

Aaron smiled. "When I'm not your social director, I'm everyone else's," he said. "I'm in charge of what Abuelo calls 'purposeful amusement.' I create games and challenges. I set up things to do when everyone gathers in Abuelo's mansion, or for the picnics on Sunday afternoon."

"So, then, you're a"—I tried to come up with the perfect word—"a *recreologist.*"

He looked at me funny, and his expression made me laugh.

"Recreologist," he said, mulling it over. "I like it. You're good with words." He held eye contact with me, and it made me uncomfortable What was it with these people? They were all gorgeous, and yet they could all stand to look at me. People simply didn't do that. Not even Momma, who could withstand my face better than anyone, was able to hold my gaze that long.

"Don't look at me like that!" I said, almost angry about it, because it defied everything I knew about myself. "Look at me like a normal person does, which is not looking at all!"

I stood up, knowing my face was getting red and blotchy. I stood at the edge of the little pond and dared to catch my reflection off the surface. I saw myself for only a few moments—my tainted, awful image—then the water defended itself as it always did, clouding over so it didn't have to reflect the likes of me. I growled in frustration.

"I wouldn't worry about that," Aaron said, seeing the sudden murkiness of the water. "It doesn't mean anything."

At that moment I wanted to throw him into the pond! "How can you say it doesn't mean anything? How many other people here fog water just by looking into it?"

"Abuelo says once you see a person's soul, you no longer see the outside."

"Abuelo's full of it!" I told him. "I'd like you a whole lot better if you just admitted, like a normal person, that I'm ugly!"

"Fine," Aaron said, getting miffed for the first time since I'd met him. "You're ugly. You're totally, completely, and undeniably ugly. If it makes you happy, I'll shout it to all of De León."

I still felt the flush in my face, but the reasons for it were changing. "It doesn't make me happy," I said quietly.

"Well," he said, offering me the slightest grin, "we'll have to find other ways to make you happy."

I can't quite say what I felt for Aaron during those first days in De León. Was it gratitude? Respect? Awe? It certainly wasn't the same kind of hopeless longing I had felt for Gerardo, and it couldn't quite be love, because I barely knew him. I liked his attention, though, and the way he treated me. Most of the good-looking people I knew were terminally self-centered, but Aaron didn't seem to be that way. He was genuine, he was thoughtful, he was too good to be true—and that kept me suspicious.

He was also very good at what he did. I got a taste of Aaron's "recreology" that first Sunday. He organized all sorts of clever races and contests—and everyone joined in, including me.

It was a Tom Sawyer kind of life in De León, and Abuelo was like our own Hispanic Mark Twain. I told Abuelo that, and he just laughed. "I am partial to Cervantes," he said, and he explained that Cervantes was the Spanish author who had written *Don Quixote,* a famous story about an old knight who did crazy things, like attack a windmill. "He thought the windmills might be giants," Abuelo said. "I applaud a madman who sees the fantastic in the ordinary."

The point is, life was frozen in De León, in a time that may never really have existed. You might be tempted to call them backward, or ignorant, but you'd be wrong. They knew and understood technology, all the conveniences of modern life, but they simply didn't need any of it. Cars? Why have a car when the valley was only a mile long, and the walk was so refreshing? Electric lights? What was the point, when candles and hearths were so much more friendly and inviting? Telephones? Why not talk face-to-face when so much of communication is body language?

There was simply nothing wrong in De León—and, like I said, that kind of perfection is highly suspect. And then, of course, there were the Seven Mysteries, which made me wonder about the place even more—but I'll get to those later.

Even with my suspicious nature, I quickly fell into the easy pace of life there, and each day I found myself thinking about my old life less and less. It's not like I forgot about my family, or Gerardo, or even Marisol and Marshall . . . but when your days are packed with people who are genuinely kind and unburdened by their own lives, how can you choose to think of bad times? The thoughts did come, though. Usually at night. I would worry about Momma worrying about me. I thought about how Dad would blame himself because of that stupid deal he'd made with Marshall about the car. I thought of Miss Leticia, and mourned the fact that I hadn't been there for her funeral. But then morning would come, Aaron would be at my door with a smile that appeared to have no ulterior motive, and those lonely night thoughts dissolved like the early-morning mist.

Getting to know everyone in De León, and seeing how well they all fit in, made it more and more obvious to me that I didn't. It was a constant reminder that I'd eventually have to leave. I didn't know where I would go, only that I couldn't go back home. I mentioned this to Aaron, and he just became uncomfortable, and shrugged. The thought of me leaving was the only thing that ever seemed to rattle him—after all, I was the only one here his age, and beggars can't be choosers.

Harmony was much more open when I talked to her about eventually leaving.

"If you find your place among us," she asked, "will you still want to leave?"

I thought about it. "No," I told her, and it was the truth—but I couldn't imagine anything I could do that would be of use to anyone in De León.

After I'd been in De León for a week, my little one-room cottage had become furnished and inviting. There was something missing, though, and I couldn't put my finger on what it could be. It was Aaron who had the insight to see what was really missing from the place.

It was the evening of my seventh day. He had just come over with a wooden board game he had invented and Willem had built for him. Kind of a cross between Stratego and chess. We had just started playing when he looked around the room, and said, "These are all things other people wanted to give you . . . but since you've been here, you haven't said if there's anything *you* want."

"Oh, I don't know," I said. "Maybe a radio? A laptop? A *TV Guide*?" But I was kidding, and he knew it. If I missed any of those things, I only missed them on the surface, because they were familiar. I thought about his question a bit more deeply. Once I did, my answer was easy. "How about a bamboo paint-brush, some ink, and some paper?"

Aaron nodded. "I'll see what I can do."

The next afternoon he came to my cottage all smiles, with a jar of ink in one hand and a brush in the other. "We didn't have bamboo," he said, "so Willem used his lathe to make you one out of birch wood."

I took the brush, holding it like something precious. The pale bristles were soft and tapered to a point, the way I liked it. I could tell it wasn't wolf hair, or even rabbit. "What kind of hair is it?"

Aaron blushed a bit, and scratched the side of his head, revealing a little thin patch on his scalp.

"No!" I said. "You didn't."

"I did. You've got yourself a genuine Aaron-hair brush."

"That's just plain creepy."

He shrugged. "It just means there'll be a little bit of me in everything you draw."

I looked at the brush again, deciding it wasn't as creepy as it was sweet. Then I realized something was missing. "Is there any paper?"

He smiled and gestured toward the empty white walls of the cottage. "Who needs paper?"

I think that was the moment my feelings toward Aaron took a quantum leap beyond gratitude, respect, and awe.

14
▲
THe seven mysteries

I once saw this documentary about a family who had adopted a young chimpanzee. They raised it as part of the family. It ate at the table, had its own room done up like any other kid's room. The little chimp had all the love it could handle, and yet there was a deep sadness in its eyes. *It knows there's something wrong,* I remember thinking. *It knows it can never be like the tall, slender creatures around it.* I wondered if he was human in his dreams, only to wake up to realize it was never going to happen.

That's how I felt among the beautiful people of De León, and no matter how accepted they made me feel, I knew I would never be like them. I wondered how long it would take for them to realize it and send me on my way.

I had been in paradise for three weeks when Abuelo paid a surprise visit to my cottage. What had begun as a bare room was now decorated with furniture, quilts, and other warm touches brought by the residents of De León. Everything, of course, but mirrors.

I was doing my ink drawings—I had already filled up two whole walls and was working on a third. I stiffened when I saw Abuelo at my open front door. Abuelo never came to visit *you—*

you always went to see *him.* I looked at the ink drawings on the wall and felt as if I had been caught doing something wrong.

"Hola, mi hija," he said as he stepped in. "I came to see how you are getting on."

"I'm good," I squeaked out. Abuelo never did anything without purpose. I was convinced that this was the day he would cast me out. After all, I had yet to make myself useful here. Was my free ride over? My heart began to beat like I was running a marathon, but I tried not to let it show.

He took a look at the walls, taking them in, saying nothing, then stepped back from the fullest wall to see it as a whole. "It looks like . . . writing," he said.

"It is . . . kind of," I explained. "I use the basic strokes of Chinese writing for all my drawing." I picked up my brush and on a blank spot of wall showed him the seven simple marks I had taught myself years ago.

"The Chinese call these strokes the Seven Mysteries," I told him.

Abuelo studied the seven marks, then stepped closer to examine the individual drawings, each one no larger than a sheet of paper, since that was the size I was used to. I waited for him to turn to me, offer his apologies, and tell me I had to leave De León. But he didn't. Instead he pointed to three of the drawings. "This one is the view from your porch," he said. "This, I think, is Harmony's garden. And this . . . this is me!" He smiled broadly. *"Qué bueno!"*

I can't tell you how relieved I was by his approval. A man who smiled like that wasn't about to hurl you back over the mountains. "You got all three right!" I said. Even though the drawings were stylized, and simplified with the barest gestures of lines, he had figured them out.

Then he turned to the one wall I hadn't gotten to yet—still stark white, without a single brushstroke. He pointed to it. "Leave this wall blank," he said. Then he nodded to me, said *adios,* and left without another word.

As relieved as I was that he hadn't expelled me from De León, I was also confused.

Leave this wall blank.

It was a mystery. The *seventh* mystery, I thought, and glanced at the individual drying brush marks on the wall. Even more than keeping track of the days, I was keeping track of the many strange things that didn't sit right with me about De León. I was supposed to "find the answers" here, but for a place that was supposed to hold all my answers, the people of De León didn't care much for my questions. Oh, sure, they were polite when I asked, but through the pleasant talk, there was a silent air of secrecy—like they all had a malformed child locked away in the attic—which was impossible, because of mystery number one: There were no children in De León.

Aaron had become uncomfortable when I asked him about it during my first days there.

"The women here don't seem to be able to have babies," he told me. "I think it's something in the water."

"That's awful."

Aaron shrugged. "They don't mind. Or at least they don't anymore."

It bothered me, but not as much as it might have, since I didn't plan on inflicting my genes on a defenseless, unsuspecting future—but how could such a thing not bother all the other women here? I asked Aaron more questions about it, but he just changed the subject.

It wasn't just him. Everyone I spoke to had the same kind of response to my questions. It was like all of their information was sifted through a strainer, to remove anything juicy before it got to me.

Mystery number two: "To Serve Abuelo."

I learned about this particular mystery while weaving with Harmony and a few of the other women, when I questioned them about the isolation of the town.

"If nothing comes in or out," I asked Harmony, "how did Abuelo send me his letter?"

The women in the room, who had seemed so happy with their weaving and their humming, now looked at one another apprehensively.

"The monastery," said one of the other women. She was immediately shushed, and the silence that fell made the birds outside seem loud.

I looked to each of them, but none would return my gaze. "Monastery?" Hadn't Abuelo once mentioned something about monks?

Harmony sighed. "We're not *entirely* self-sufficient," she said. "Our valley is small. We don't have land to raise our crops, or to raise livestock. So Abuelo struck a bargain a very long time ago with the Vladimirian monks."

I thought of the various kinds of monks I knew about. Buddhist. Franciscan. Benedictine.

"I never heard of the Vladimirian monks," I told them.

"And you never will hear of them again," a woman named Gertrude said. "They exist to keep us secret. To bring us the food we cannot grow, and to take messages to the outside world when we need it."

"And what do they get out of it?"

"The joy of serving Abuelo," Gertrude said.

"And," said Harmony, "that's all there is to know about that." Then she launched into a song, and the other women joined in. Although I had a ton more questions, it was clear there were no more answers in this sewing circle.

Mystery number three: "Go with the Flow."

I stumbled upon this one while visiting with Claude and Willem, the two men who made furniture. I enjoyed watching them work, and I loved the smell of the fresh wood—but I had a better reason for hanging around them. Unlike many of the others, they got careless with their talk—especially once they grew more comfortable with me.

"How long have you lived here?" I once asked them as they worked together on a table.

"Not all that long," the tall one named Willem said. "Our little group is nomadic by nature."

"Nomadic?" I said. "It seems to me you've been here for a long time."

"*Long* is a relative word," said Claude, with a distinctly French accent. "We were in Lourdes before this. And before that Tibet— a valley in the Himalayas, not much different than this, although even less accessible."

"We follow the flow," said Willem.

"The flow of what?"

The question hit a nerve, and they both became a bit uncomfortable.

"Just the flow."

I knew I had stumbled upon something important, but what it meant, I had no idea. "So how much longer will you be staying here?" I asked.

Willem rubbed his hand thoughtfully on the smooth wood of the tabletop. "Abuelo seems to think it won't be much longer. But I think he might be wrong." Then he looked out the window. "Just look at that grass. Look how rich it is, look how green."

Claude shook his head without looking up from his work. "He was right the last time."

"Yes. Well, we'll see." And then Willem changed the subject. "Have you considered what your place might be here? What you can add to our little community?"

"That's easy," I told him. "Nothing."

"Pshaw," he said. "I'm sure you'll think of something." I never actually heard a person say "pshaw" before. I almost laughed.

"You must have some skills."

I shrugged. "I can spell."

"Ooh," said Claude, "witchcraft! We have no witches here. That would be new."

"No." I sighed, thinking about poor Miss Leticia, who had made the same mistake. "Not that kind of spell. I spell words."

Willem rubbed his chin thoughtfully, getting sawdust all over it. "Hmm. Words, words, words . . . we already have a poet."

"And a scribe."

"Ah, well," said Willem, this time with less conviction. "I'm sure you'll find something."

Mystery number four was the weather, and mystery number five was everything that grew beneath the unseasonably warm sun. See, it was almost winter now. Back in Flock's Rest, sycamores would have lost all their leaves; the days would be cold and the nights colder. But in De León, it was always spring on the edge of summer.

I asked Petra, our resident piano virtuoso, about it, and she answered without missing a single note in her sonata. "It's the pattern of winds, and thermal vents in the mountainside," she said. "I think it's called a microclimate. I'm sure there are books about it in Abuelo's library."

I looked, but I couldn't find a single one.

The fishing pond was mystery number six. Soren was De León's designated fisherman—a big Scandinavian with a blond beard that hid most of his face. He would have looked natural in a Viking hat.

I stopped to watch him fish one day and asked how such a small pond—no bigger than thirty yards across—could support so many fish, and so many different varieties.

The utter panic in the big man's eyes at the question was almost comical. "I just catch them," he mumbled.

"Still, I'll bet you have a theory about it."

Again, panic. Then he was saved by a tug on his line. "Excuse me." He reeled in his catch. I don't know much about fish, but I do know that I'd never seen anything like this one before. It was at least two feet long, with a blood-red head, fading to a neon-blue body, blending into a tail as green as the oak leaves shading the pond from the unseasonably warm sun. It made me think of the Galápagos Islands—a place off the coast of South America so isolated, it gave rise to creatures seen nowhere else in the world.

"So," I said, gaping at the unearthly fish, "is that what they mean by a 'rainbow trout'?"

He quickly strung up his fish with the other equally odd specimens he had caught, said "good day," and left like a man racing from a tornado.

And now I had mystery number seven: an order from Abuelo to leave a perfectly good drawing wall untouched, with no explanation. Perhaps it was less grand then the other mysteries, but it was just as frustrating. They all knew things I didn't—I was certain of it. It was all a reminder that I was the chimp at the table.

The day after Abuelo's surprise visit, Aaron came to take me out for a picnic. I knew right away that this was different from the other times we had done things together. I could tell because he was apprehensive, maybe a little bit excited. *This is a date,* I thought. The only other date I'd been on was that infamous and miserable night with Marshall Astor—but this was something else entirely. I didn't know whether I was more excited or terrified.

Aaron led me from my end of the valley to the other, where Abuelo's mansion stood, then he took me up the steep slope behind it, as if we were climbing out of the valley.

"Where are we going?" I asked.

"You'll see."

The soft grass gave way to harsh nettles as we got higher, and soon the rough brush gave way to jagged rocks. The valley was not easy to get out of, or to get into, for that matter.

The shoes they had given me were not meant for climbing this kind of terrain. I wanted to ask Aaron where we were going, but he had this look on his face—a slight grin of anticipation, and I could tell that whatever he wanted to show me, it was a surprise.

Finally, Aaron stopped at a plateau, the mountainside still looming ahead of us.

"Have a look," he said, then gently grabbed my shoulders and turned me around.

I hadn't realized how high we had climbed until I looked out to see the valley spread before us.

On either side of the valley were dense clouds. I could hear distant thunder and see lightning flashes within the grayness. It was storming in the outside world, but the clouds never flowed over those hillsides into the valley of De León.

We sat down and ate sandwiches made from home-cured ham and fresh-baked bread. My clothes had gotten dirty from the climb, but I noticed that Aaron's didn't have a trace of dust. I reached over and touched his sleeve. I did it to feel the fabric, but then I realized I was gently rubbing his arm. I pulled my hand back, a bit embarrassed.

"No, it's okay," he said. "You like the way it feels, don't you? It's made of swan gossamer."

I looked at him like I hadn't heard him correctly. "Swan what?"

"Swan gossamer," he said. "Once a year the swans come in the spring to mate. Hundreds of them. We brush through their feathers to collect the soft down, and then spin it into thread."

"It's so beautiful."

"It never gets dirty. It never wears out."

"I wish I could wear it," I said.

He smiled at that, then reached up and touched my face, looking, as he always did, right into my eyes. It would have been a wonderfully romantic moment, but my face, which had always been my enemy, chose this moment to launch an offensive—and when I say offensive, I truly do mean *offensive*.

They say acne is caused by pores swelling up, becoming infected. When a pore is clogged with dirt, it becomes a blackhead. As the infection grows, it becomes a whitehead. And every once in a while, one of them turns into Mount St. Helens. If you have acne, you know exactly what I mean. And if you don't, just be thankful.

Aaron quickly pulled his hand away when he realized he had inadvertently popped a zit. For a brief, brief instant, he looked at me with the same nauseated disgust that I got from the rest of the world. Then he looked away from me for a moment, forcing that feeling away. He wiped his fingers on a rock. "Don't worry about it," he said. "It happens."

I couldn't look at him now. I was too humiliated. I pressed the back of my hand to my face, just in case I wasn't done erupting. I felt tears of embarrassment coming, so I let my hair dangle in front of my face so he couldn't see it.

"No," he said, sounding a little bit angry. "Don't you do that. Look at me."

I shook my head. What a fool I was to think that I could have anything resembling a normal relationship with someone who looked like Aaron. All my weeks here, pretending I could ever belong—but I was just deluding myself—and the people here weren't helping, they were just feeding that delusion—even Aaron. As he sat across from me, I realized he was just taking the mercy seat. The school cafeteria was gone, but the mercy seat would always be there no matter where I was.

Then Aaron said, "You don't remember me, do you?"

That made me look up. "Remember you?"

"I thought you eventually would, but you didn't. Maybe this will help." He brought his hands to his face. "I don't know if I can do it anymore. It's been a while, but I'll try."

He put his thumbs behind his ears and pushed them forward so they stuck out like funnels. With his index fingers, he lifted up on his eyebrows. With his pinkies, he pulled down on his cheeks, so his eyes took on a mournful droop. He sucked his cheeks in, pushed his lower jaw out so that his bottom teeth stuck out in an underbite. Then he pushed his lips forward and pursed them so they looked like a pink hair scrunchie.

Suddenly it hit me.

"Tuddie?"

He let go of his ears and his eyes and put his jaw back in its natural position.

"That nickname stuck so well," he said, "no one even knew my real name was Aaron."

I looked at that face, that beautiful face, and although I could see a hint of the resemblance to That Ugly Dude, as everyone called him, it was hard to believe this was the same boy. I'd be lying if I said I could recognize him from his eyes, because back home I never looked into Tuddie's eyes. No one did.

"But . . . your face . . ." I said. "How . . . ?"

Aaron just shrugged. "You could say I grew out of my awkward stage."

Then he told me how he had run away, much the same way I had, at that defining moment when he could no longer stand how he was treated. He was on the run for months, until he found this place.

"I dreamed about it, though," he told me. "I knew the direction I had to go, but I had no hints to help me along. It took a while, but I finally found my way here. At first Abuelo wasn't going to let me stay. He said I was too young. This society didn't have room for people our age—but you see, they were getting bored. One party, one picnic, had gotten just like every other. So I started making up new things for them to do. Abuelo chose to let me stay . . . then I thought of you."

Now I couldn't look him in the face again, but this time for a different reason. A different kind of shame.

"Why would you think of me? I was so nasty to you."

"So was everyone," said Aaron.

"But coming from me, it must have been worse."

"It was. But after a while I stopped blaming you for it. See, Cara, I understand. I know what it's like to hate your face so much, you wish you could be out of your own skin. And so when you looked at me, how could you help but hate me, when I only reminded you of yourself?"

His unconditional forgiveness made me feel less deserving of it. "Well, as you can see," I said bitterly, "I have *not* grown out of my awkward phase, and all your charity isn't going to change it."

"You know what your problem is? You spent too much time listening to all those idiots in Flock's Rest who made you feel worthless. That girl—what was her name? Marissa?"

"Marisol," I said, growling it out like it was a foul word.

"You still think about her, and all the others, don't you?"

"Sometimes."

"Well, don't! I never think about any of them—not at all. Because I am *not* Tuddie anymore, and you don't have to be the Flock's Rest Monster!"

"Tell it to the mirrors!"

I realized I was shouting, and I looked down, even if he didn't want me to. "I'm sorry," I said. "It's not you I'm mad at."

"So who are you mad at?"

"I don't know. Everyone? No one? God?" I reached up the sleeve of my dress to blot my tears. And the fabric got stained, not just with tears, but with a spot of yuck still oozing from my popped zit. "Let's just go back," I said, disgusted. "Picnic's over."

But he didn't move. Instead he said: "I know something that'll help your acne."

"No, you don't," I told him. "Nothing can help it. Believe me, I've tried everything."

And then he whispered, "You haven't tried this."

Aaron got up and began to climb higher up the steep, rocky slope behind us. "C'mon," he said. "It's not far." Then, when I didn't move, he said, "Or are you just gonna sit there and feel sorry for yourself?"

That got me moving. Like I said, I didn't like to wallow in self-pity, and here I was doing just that. "Okay," I said, "wait up."

After only about two minutes of climbing, we came to a deep crack in the mountain face. I could feel warm air rising from its depths and smell earth, like in the first moments of a rainstorm. This wasn't just a crack in the stone, this was the mouth of a cave.

Aaron stepped into the darkness, but I hesitated. Standing in the stark daylight, I couldn't see him in the cave ahead of me, but I heard his voice coming from inside. Now, without seeing his face, just hearing his voice, I truly recognized him as the boy I once knew as Tuddie.

"I can't force you to follow me," he said. "You have to come because you want to."

Want. There were a lot of things I wanted right then. Too many to put into words. I was a big empty bucket of *want*.

"You've trusted me this far," he said from the darkness. "Will you trust me a little bit farther?"

There was something important about all of this. Then it occurred to me that being at the mouth of this cave was no coincidence. Whatever was down there in that cave was the reason we came all the way up this mountainside for the picnic.

M-O-M-E-N-T-O-U-S.

I felt like I did when I stood in my room, before my mirror, daring myself to tear away the sheet. Spelling the words in my head always helped move me forward.

D-E-C-I-S-I-V-E.

One step more, and I entered the mouth of the cave.

D-E-S-T-I-N-Y.

I reached into the darkness, felt Aaron grab my hand, and he pulled me out of the light and into the bowels of the earth.

15

▲

THE CAULDRON OF LIFE

We lingered in darkness for a moment, then I heard the *whoosh* of a flame, and I could see his face again, lit in orange flickering light. In one hand he held a torch.

When my eyes adjusted to the dim light of the cave, I could see a narrow slope leading deeper into the mountain. He didn't speak as he led the way down.

"What's down here?" I asked.

"Best to see for yourself."

We went through one cavern after another, and when I thought we had reached the bottom, there was yet another deep, winding pathway taking us farther down.

"Stay close to the light," he said when I started to lag too far behind. "There are things living down here."

"What kinds of things?"

"They don't have names—but they won't come near the light."

I tried to imagine what could possibly live here beside bats and rats, but my imagination hadn't prepared me for the "things" Aaron was talking about.

We rounded a bend, and only for a moment I saw it scuttle up a wall and out of sight. It looked something like a koala, with soft, furry eyes, a small snout . . . and eight spidery legs that clung to the wall as it scurried away. I groaned slightly. Seeing that was more information than I needed, and from that moment on I stayed as close to the light as I could possibly get. Even Aaron seemed frightened by it, but only slightly—or maybe he was only being brave for me.

"No one's ever been hurt by the things down here."

"Always a first time," I told him.

The caverns, which began as empty stone chambers, slowly began to change their nature the deeper we got. Massive stone formations, almost bonelike in shape, stretched from floor to ceiling around us. Stalagmites grew from the ground like jagged teeth, and stalactites dangled from above us like limestone icicles. They all shimmered like they were covered with diamond dust, reflecting Aaron's torch in every color of the rainbow. The fear I had when I began our descent was slowly replaced by wonder.

Finally, we reached the most magnificent cavern of all, and Aaron doused the torch because he didn't need it anymore. The walls themselves were glowing, giving off a strange light as bright as moonlight on snow. It was hot and humid here; my clothes stuck to my body, and yet it wasn't an unpleasant sensation. The air hung motionless, smelling like mint and eucalyptus and cinnamon wrapped together in a rich earthy peat. Miss Leticia would have liked this place.

Aaron spoke in a whisper, but here the softest voice sounded loud. "Abuelo says God needed a cauldron to brew up creation, and here it is. We call this cavern *El Caldero de Vida*—the Cauldron of Life. After He was done, God might have cast the cauldron aside, but it's never entirely empty."

We walked forward into the cavern. The floor was covered with moss greener than the grass in the valley. I couldn't imagine anything green growing down here, about a mile down, and yet it did.

"Take off your shoes," Aaron said.

As I remembered from my days in Sunday school, that's what Moses had to do when he approached the Burning Bush. "Why?" I asked. "Is this holy ground?"

Aaron shrugged. "Maybe." Then he smiled. "But I just like the feel of the moss on my feet." He was right about that. Once I took off my shoes, it felt like I was walking on plush green velvet.

"Abuelo believes the earth itself is a living thing, and this is where its soul lives." Looking at this place, I could see why the old man felt that way.

"Do you believe that?" I asked.

Aaron thought about the question and, rather than answering, said, "Abuelo is sometimes very crazy, and sometimes very wise. It's hard to figure out which is which."

We stepped forward across the massive domed cavern. In the very center, hanging from the ceiling, was a single stalactite, tapering down from the roof and coming to a pinpoint about ten feet above the floor. It was glistening wet, and I got a shiver, because it reminded me of something, and I didn't know what. I stopped walking, but Aaron gently took my elbow and urged me forward.

I slowly approached the great glistening stalactite. The only sound now was the squelch of my feet against the soft moss and a rhythmic drip of water. Suddenly it occurred to me what the stalactite reminded me of.

An uvula. That strange dangle of skin at the back of your throat.

Beneath it was a stone formation growing from the cavern floor. It looked like a pedestal widening into a basin, like a birdbath just a foot or so wide, full of water. Moisture had collected on the stalactite, and every five seconds or so a single drop of water fell from the tip into the basin, with a delicate *plink*. The sound was like the faintest, highest note struck on a xylophone.

There was a mist across the surface of that little pool of water. The closer I got, the more I could feel its heat.

Plink.

"Mineral water," Aaron said. "Just what your face needs. It'll open those pores and get rid of that acne."

"You think so?"

"Oh," said Aaron, "I *know* so."

Plink.

Then he put his finger in and swirled it around. "It's just right," he said. "Body temperature." The steam cleared away as he stirred, and colors played in the water like the aurora borealis—the northern lights captured in a shallow stone bowl. When he took his finger out, he wiped the water beneath one of his eyes, and then the other, as if it were invisible war paint. Then he licked his fingertip.

Plink.

The surface of the water was glassy, and for a strange instant I had the impression that someone was in there looking out at me, until I realized that it was my own reflection. I was just as horrible as ever. There was mustard on my lip from our lunch, and smudges of dirt from touching my face after touching the cavern walls. It was the longest I'd ever been able to see my own reflection, because *this* water did not cloud.

Plink.

"Go on," Aaron whispered, standing right behind me now. Then he brought his lips as close to my ear as he could without actually touching it and whispered, "Your face is dirty. Wash it off."

Plink.

Between one drop of water and the next, I dipped both my hands deep into the pool and splashed the water onto my face. Once. Twice. Three times.

It burned. Not like the heat of water, not like the heat of flames, but a different kind of heat that soaked in through my pores, like fine needles penetrating so deep I could feel it all the way to the tips of my toes.

I opened my eyes, thinking they would sting, but they didn't. And when I looked at my hands, the water had already dried up, absorbed into the dryness of my skin.

"There," said Aaron. "All your skin needed was a good deep cleaning. No more acne for you."

The shimmering lights were gone from the pool, and it had misted over again. Another drop plunged from the pointy tip of the stalactite into the stone bowl.

Plink.

"Come on, Cara," Aaron said. "Let's go home."

16
▲
UNVEILING

It was already dusk when we emerged from the caverns, and by the time we made it back down into the valley, the sun was long gone from the sky.

There was a celebration at Abuelo's mansion when we got back. The entire population of De León was there. This time they weren't scattered around the mansion as I'd seen them before. Tonight, everyone was in that great room at the top of the stairs.

Musicians played, and people danced. Harmony was the first to hurry to me, and she gave me a bone-crunching hug.

"It's so good to finally *see* you," she said.

"What do you mean?" I asked her. "I just saw you yesterday."

"Let me take you to Abuelo," she said. "I know he'll want to see you right away."

We weaved through the dancing couples. The band played a melody that was a strange cross between classical and swing. I had never heard that piece of music before, and wondered if it had been written by one of the citizens in the town.

I looked around for Aaron, but he had already dissolved into the crowd behind me, and then, as we moved through the couples spinning one another to the music, there was Abuelo, on his settee.

Next to him was an intravenous stand, and a plastic bag of clear fluid dripped down a narrow tube that went into the vein on his left arm.

I had seen this before, on my own grandfather, when he was dying in the hospital. However, this old man seemed in the best of health. Truth be told, he seemed more radiant than any other time I'd seen him.

"What's the matter, Abuelo?" I asked. "Are you sick?"

He found this amusing, and turned to a woman beside him who was not quite as old as he. They shared a look and a chuckle. It irritated me that I couldn't be in on their little joke.

"I am, as you say, fit as a fiddle. Even fitter, for a fiddle will break its strings, whereas I will not."

He saw me looking at the intravenous bag.

"Oh, this thing. It's just a little pick-me-up. My annual beauty treatment." He and everyone within listening distance laughed.

He called to the musicians to stop playing, and they did almost instantly. The dancing couples turned around to see what was happening, and as Abuelo stood, they cleared the floor.

He went out to the center of the room, rolling his intravenous stand with him. "My dance partner is slender and graceful, no?" Then he turned to me and gestured with one hand. "Come."

I didn't like being ordered around like a dog, and I didn't like being the center of attention. I felt the way I had beneath the lights at the spelling bee, but with the eyes of everyone in the room on me, I had no choice. I thought about the ritual of flowers when I first arrived, and wondered if some other ritual was in store for me today. Was today the day I would be cast out? Had they grown tired of looking at me?

The old man put his hands onto my shoulders, like a real grandfather might, and looked into my eyes.

"Ah, my ugly one, my ugly one. Do you have any idea at all who I am?"

Although I had no idea, I was beginning to sense that the answer was not something I was prepared to hear. Not just because of the cunning twinkle in his eye, but because I chanced to look at the intravenous bag hanging beside him and noticed something I hadn't noticed before. The clear water inside wasn't entirely clear. It was swimming with faint colors like the northern lights.

"My given name is Juan," Abuelo said. "My family name is Ponce de León."

I rolled it over in my mind. Juan Ponce de León—one of the great Spanish explorers. "You're one of his descendants?"

Abuelo slowly shook his head. "Think again."

As I recalled, Juan Ponce de León had laid claim to Florida—but he was best known for his folly, which was searching all his life for something he never found.

Or had he?

I thought back to the mineral pool deep in the "Cauldron of Life."

"The Fountain of Youth!" I said out loud.

It made the old man smile.

"You see," he said, to all those assembled, "every schoolchild knows of me."

"But that's impossible! That would make you hundreds of years old . . ."

"Five hundred and forty-six—but who's counting?" He laughed heartily. "Alas, I found the fountain too late in life to be eternally young. Instead I am eternally old. It could not restore me, only sustain me, keeping me at the same age I was when I first partook of its waters. But I am not bitter—for I have learned that youth is overrated. It is the fountain's other gift— its *true* gift that I have come to value far more than youth."

Now I was beginning to feel like the butt of an elaborate joke. "You expect me to believe this?"

"Believe what you like," Abuelo said. "Believe that the moon is cheese, the world is flat, and that I am just a crazy old man." Then he smiled, cupping my face in his hands. I wanted to back away, but I was transfixed by his eyes. "And now, my little mud hen, time for the unveiling."

He turned and shouted, "Uncover them!"

Then people all around the room, standing close to the walls, turned and tore off the white satiny cloths that covered the mirrors. Suddenly light zigzagged in paths across the room from one mirror to another. Those mirrors were everywhere. There was nowhere I could look without seeing one. I closed my eyes and knelt on the floor, covering my face.

"Please don't do this," I said, my voice not much more than a whimper. "Don't you know what will happen?"

But the old man gently helped me up and moved me toward the mirrors. I still couldn't look at them.

"Come now, Cara," he said. "These mirrors will not hate you. They want to love you. Every one of them. Look at yourself."

I lifted my eyes to see my reflection, still believing that the mirror would shatter.

And the person I saw looking back was not me at all.

This face in the mirror—it could have been a relative: a sister

I never had. The opposite of me. This reflection had my mother's graceful cheekbones, my father's soft eyes. A face with all the good genes that had been denied me was now peering at me through eyes that were perfectly shaped.

I reached up to touch my face. My skin was clear. No rashes, no pimples, no boils. Smooth and soft as the skin of a peach.

"You see?" said Abuelo. "The fire of beauty now burns within you."

I looked around for an explanation, but all I could see was everyone smiling at me. Happy for me. And most of all, Aaron.

Abuelo, still holding my shoulders, stood behind me as we gazed into the mirror together.

"The fountain's greatest gift is the gift of eternal beauty. There is a legend that the Angel of Death is beautiful, and she will never take the life of anyone more beautiful than she. This, I believe, is why we here in De León live forever. Not because the fountain makes us eternal, but because true beauty never dies."

I couldn't take my eyes off of myself. It was the first time I could truly look at my reflection. How could I be this beautiful creature?

Then I heard a gentle voice behind me. "I have something for you." It was Harmony. I turned to see her unfolding a dress. Simple, clean, and, like all of their clothes, made from swan gossamer.

The old man stepped back, the women surrounded me, and there, within the cocoon of the women of De León, they took off my cotton dress and clothed me in the velvety white garments of the eternally beautiful. I felt like a bride.

Soon the band started up again, the room so much brighter now with all the mirrors. It seemed to be filled with a thousand people instead of just a hundred. Everyone danced in circles, catching their own gazes in the mirrors that had been covered since the day I arrived.

I danced with everyone who came for my hand, but mostly I danced with Aaron.

When the celebration was over, I walked back with him, arm in arm, down the winding path to my little cottage on the opposite end of the valley. Perhaps it was still the effect of the water, but I felt like I was hovering over the ground in a daze. I was myself, yet I was *not* myself, and it felt wonderful.

He left me at my door with a kiss. This was nothing like that awful kiss I had stolen from Marshall Astor on homecoming night. Aaron's kiss was as perfect as he was. As we both were.

"You're truly one of us now," he said. "You always have been, you just didn't know it."

After he left, I closed the door, took off my beautiful dress, and slipped beneath the covers, for the first time feeling sheets against skin that wasn't pocked like the surface of the moon—a moon that, for all I knew, really was made of cheese, because all the rules that had made up the world I knew were now in serious question. Life was suddenly magical and full of wonder.

Right here, right now is my "happily ever after" moment, I thought. I would have been perfectly happy for time to stop and the universe to come to a satisfied end.

But, of course, it didn't.

17

POSTMORTALITY

I won't try to explain what it's like to go from hideous to gorgeous. There are no words to describe the feeling—at least not in any language I knew . . . or at least any language I knew *yet*. Let's just say Miss Leticia had been right all along. I did have a destiny.

In those first days after the unveiling, I soaked in my new self, just as my skin had soaked in the water of the fountain. It was amazing how many mirrors there really were in De León, once they had all been uncovered—and I must have caught my reflection in every one, preening like a model for the camera. I know it sounds awful, but I just couldn't help it. It's like I needed to see that beautiful reflection over and over again to make myself believe it was real. Hair like mocha silk; soulful caramel eyes; skin as smooth as my swan-gossamer gown; and a figure with all the right curves from whatever angle you looked.

I posed for Giancarlo, the portrait painter. "Venus herself would be jealous," he said, and Abuelo promised to hang the portrait in his mansion once it dried.

I visited everyone, spoke with everyone in De León those first few days, and if I had questions before, I had even more now. This time, though, everyone was much freer with their answers . . . although they all acted as if the answers should be obvious.

"If it's the Fountain of Youth and Beauty, why isn't everyone young?" I asked Aaron as I helped him prepare for a treasure hunt that would take the citizens of De León most of Sunday to complete.

"Nearest I can figure is that the water doesn't move time *backward,* it just stops it where it is. Whatever state you were when you drank, that's where you stay."

"So I'll always be sixteen?" I asked.

He laughed. "It doesn't stop you from growing, silly—just from growing old."

I didn't quite get it, until I remembered something I had learned in science—that there's a point for everyone where they stop growing *up,* and start growing *old.* "I think girls are supposed to keep growing until they're about eighteen," I said. "But boys grow until they're about twenty."

"So there you go," said Aaron. "We'll be eighteen and twenty forever. Once we get there, of course."

I laughed. Even the sound of my laugh had changed, filtered through a much more shapely mouth. Aaron looked at me and shook his head. "What is it?" I asked.

"Nothing. It's just that for all those weeks, I tried to imagine what you'd look like after visiting the fountain. I never even came close to imagining you the way you look now."

"What if it hadn't worked?" I asked him. "What if I had stayed ugly?"

"Why would you want to think about something like that?"

He grabbed me and tickled me in the ribs until I laughed, and forgot the question.

During one of my weaving sessions with Harmony and her friends, I asked about children again. I wanted to find out for myself whether the women of De León truly didn't mind being barren.

"Nature gives life in many ways," she said. "There can't be birth without death."

Gertrude nodded. "It would be unnatural."

It seemed strange to me that she would say something like that—after all, there was nothing natural about eternal life, was there? But then, if the fountain was a natural place, perhaps it was. Perhaps it was just a hidden side of nature.

"There are times I wish I could trade postmortality for the chance to have children," said one of the younger women. "But that's not a choice we have anymore. Postmortality is forever."

"Don't you mean *immortality*?" I said.

Harmony strung a fresh thread of gossamer into her loom before answering. "Abuelo might talk of immortality, but none of us is truly immortal, Cara. We *can* live forever, but that doesn't necessarily mean that we *will*."

"I . . . don't understand."

"Flesh is still flesh," she explained. "We do not wither, but we do wear. We bruise, we bleed, we break, and if it's bad enough, we die."

"That's why we have to be careful," Gertrude said, and then went into the long tale of poor Virgil Meeks, who was gored by a mountain goat and died at the untimely age of 137.

I thought about this. "It's actually a blessing that the fountain doesn't make us truly immortal," I pointed out. "I mean, what's the value of life if you can't die? How could you ever appreciate anything? This way life is still precious."

"Postmortality," like everything else in De León, was perfect—but there was still something about it that bothered me. "*Postmortality* is such an ugly word for such a wonderful thing," I told them. "Shouldn't it be called something better . . . like . . . oh, I don't know . . . *Eternessence.*"

They all chuckled and repeated the word, trying it on for size. They liked it. They liked me. Now I had not only their acceptance, but their approval as well.

I had finally stepped into that great destiny Miss Leticia had spoken of—and my destiny was perfection. But what happens once you've arrived at that final destination? What then?

I should have stayed content to be one of the beautiful people of De León, but each night, it wasn't the sense of belonging that filled me as I drifted off to sleep. More and more, my mind was filled with the faces of the people back home in Flock's Rest.

"It's natural to think about them at first," Aaron said. "Don't worry, it'll pass."

I believed him, but I had my doubts.

Abuelo called for me two weeks after my "unveiling." We met in his great ballroom. His throne room, now filled with a hundred mirrors: a grand *reflectorium*. Those mirrors would stay uncovered until the next poor unnaturally ugly soul found his or her way under Abuelo's wings—and I would probably be the one to lead the new arrival down the gauntlet of flowers, as Aaron had led me.

Abuelo rose from his golden sofa and gave me a powerful hug. Then he walked around me, looking me over like I was a sculpture and he was Michelangelo.

"Harmony does good work, no? That gossamer gown is the finest she's made yet."

"It's beautiful," I said.

"Much love went into it. She has a special place in her heart for you, I think. Like a mother."

That made me think of Momma. Was Harmony taking her place? Was it okay to let that happen? One thought led to another, and in an instant my head was flooded with Flock's Rest.

"You are restless," Abuelo said. "I see this. And I also know why."

"You do?"

"It is because you have not found your place here. You have not yet found a task that fits you. Am I right in thinking this?"

I nodded, because he was half-right. I still hadn't found a purpose among the people here. It seemed to me all the good jobs were taken.

"I think I know something you can do for us. Something that will fill the coming years of your splendid *eternessence.*"

I looked at him at the sound of my made-up word, a little embarrassed. He laughed when he saw my reaction, then he opened his arms as if to hug me, but instead spun around, and in the mirrors, his many reflections spun with him. "All this," he said. "All you see in the valley, it is a world unto itself. Do you not think so?"

I nodded.

"Well," he said, "a world needs a language, don't you agree? The people here come from all over the world. We speak English now because we are here in America, but we may not always be here. What we need is a language of our own. The most beautiful language in the world, like diamonds rolling off the tips of our tongues. I would like you to create this language for us."

My breath was taken away by the request. Create an entire language? Spelling was one thing, but this? "I can't do something like that!"

"You can," Abuelo said, with absolute certainty. "Because everything about you is beauty now. Your face, your voice, and the works of your hands. You will build us this language, and then you will teach us all to speak it . . . and to write it." Then he reached into his pocket and pulled out a fresh bottle of ink, which he put into my hand. He had asked me to leave one wall of my cottage blank—now I understood why. But even so, creating a language was more than just inventing symbols and painting them on a wall. There was grammar and structure—languages grew over eons. No one person ever created an entire language.

"But . . . it'll take years."

"Indeed," he said. "Hundreds, perhaps. And now that you have been cleansed by the waters of the fountain, you have all the time you need."

And I realized he was right. Any task could be completed if there was enough time! "Thank you, Abuelo," I said, genuinely grateful, and excited about the task.

Then he kissed me on the forehead and turned me loose to begin.

I could have left Abuelo's right then. I should have—I was inspired—I was ennobled by this monumental task . . . but I hesitated. Abuelo had always treated me with kindness and wisdom. If there was anyone I could ask about things, it was him.

I turned back to him. "Abuelo, I've been thinking more and more about the people back home."

His face lost a bit of its eternescent glow. Immediately I was sorry I had said anything. "You have only one home," he said. "Your *true* home. The place you came from—that is nothing more than the broken shell out of which you were born. A worthless thing to be ground into the earth and forgotten. Do you understand?"

"Yes, Abuelo." I left, vowing never to bring it up to him again.

I spent the rest of the day in my cottage, beginning to lay ink on the white wall. I wasn't bound by the seven strokes of Chinese writing, or even the twenty-six letters of English—I could do anything. I tapped into my inner self and began to experiment with shapes and swirls of a brand-new alphabet—and it was beautiful! It was true when Abuelo had said everything about me was beauty now, right down to my brushstrokes. I created sweeping patterns of motion, carving up the white wall.

Yet even in the joy and absolute freedom of this wonderful task, unwanted thoughts kept sparking up, like shocks from a faulty circuit. Thoughts like, *Momma would be so proud of me,* or *Marisol would be so jealous,* or *Gerardo would be so impressed.*

I hurled my brush across the room in frustration. It hit the wall and left an orphan comma. I didn't even know why I should care about Flock's Rest. I had a new family, I had new friends. I had Aaron, who was better than Gerardo in every possible way, and no room in my life for enemies like Marisol.

It's natural, Aaron had said. *It'll pass.*

And so I took a deep breath and didn't fight the thoughts. I let them come, waiting for the day they would go away. But they didn't. Instead they grew like weeds in a garden—and as any gardener can tell you, the only way to get out deep weeds is to go to the root.

"You can't."

"Who says?"

"You just can't," said Aaron, pacing the width of my cottage. "Those are the rules!"

"I want a reason," I told him. "If I had a reason, maybe I could accept it. Maybe."

Aaron threw up his hands. "Why can't you be happy with what you have here? It's more than you ever had in Flock's Rest, more than you ever *could* have there!"

"I don't want to leave," I told him. "I just want to visit. I want to go back and say good-bye. I owe my parents that much!"

"No one leaves!" he insisted. "And if Abuelo found out you were talking about doing it, he'd be furious!"

Aaron stormed away, then stormed right back. Frustration bordering on anger flared in his eyes. "I never should have told Abuelo to send you that note! I should have just forgotten about you, just like I forgot about everyone else!"

It stung to hear him say something like that, and I thought maybe there was still some ugliness in De León after all.

"I'm sorry," he said, after a moment. "I didn't mean it." But the damage had already been done.

Then I turned to see Harmony standing in the doorway. I was so used to leaving my door open, I hadn't thought to close it.

"May I come in?" she asked.

I nodded. I thought to pretend like nothing was happening here, but I realized that would be pointless. "So I guess you heard everything . . ."

She sat down in one of the chairs Willem and Claude had made for me and gestured to two of the others. "Come sit down. Both of you."

I pulled up a chair, and Aaron reluctantly did, too.

"Please talk some sense into her," Aaron said.

"It's not sense she needs," Harmony said. "It's perspective."

I didn't like being talked about in third person. "So are both of you going to run to Abuelo and tell him I was talking treason? Does he have a torture chamber beneath that mansion of his? Maybe something from the Spanish Inquisition?"

"Of course not," Harmony said with a calm to her voice that just made me feel even more tense.

"Hasn't *anyone* ever left this place?"

"No!" said Aaron. "Never!"

But Harmony put up her hand to silence him. She took a long moment to think before giving me her answer, and then she began a tale she probably hadn't told for hundreds of years, if she'd ever told it at all. Her answer to my question was a thread as finely woven as her gossamer garments.

"I was one of the first settlers with Abuelo," she told us. "I've followed him from San Juan, to Tibet, to Lourdes, to this valley—and when the waters shift and the fountain moves elsewhere, I will follow Abuelo to that new place, too.

"The first time, when the fountain started to fail and we prepared to journey from San Juan, I feared that Abuelo was wrong.

The fountain had grown shallow, our little hidden rain forest was dying—and I was convinced that the fountain was drying up forever. Abuelo said he could feel the pull—he knew where the fountain would next appear, but I didn't believe him . . . so I ran away. I went back to my family in the American colonies. And do you know what I found?"

"What?" I asked.

"My sister had died of old age. My nephews and nieces were all older than me. The world had moved on, and there was no place for me. I raced back to San Juan, as quickly as travel in those days allowed, certain that Abuelo and the others would be gone . . . and as I traveled, an illness overtook me. A fever that I was sure would kill me."

"A fever?" Aaron said. "That can't be. Once you've been touched by the fountain, you can't get sick—Abuelo told us so!"

"There is one sickness we can get."

"What is it?" I asked.

Harmony thought carefully about her answer. "Consumption," she said—but by the look on her face, I had a feeling it wasn't the same kind of consumption you read about in medical books. "Luck was with me," Harmony said. "When I arrived at our little settlement, they hadn't yet left. My illness passed, Abuelo forgave me, and we sailed across the sea. I made the harsh journey with them across the Himalayas, and I was the first one to see the new valley. Once I saw the valley, I knew that I would never doubt Abuelo again."

"I've only been here a few months," I reminded her. "The world may have moved on for you, but not for me. My family is still there."

"That is true," Harmony said. "But it still doesn't mean there's a place for you in that world."

"I don't want a place," I told her. "I only want to say good-bye."

"Even so, it won't bring you any happiness."

Then Aaron spoke up again, more gently this time. "I don't want you to go. It's a hard journey, and a hundred things can go wrong." He took both my hands. "In a while you won't care anyway," he said. "That place, and those people, will feel like part of someone else's life."

I knew he was right about that. "Maybe that's why I want to do it now."

Harmony considered it, and Aaron didn't seem so much angry now as scared—scared for me, or maybe just scared of losing me. "If I'm ever going to be happy here," I told him, "I have to see my family one last time." But the more I thought about it, the more I realized there was more to it. It wasn't just that I wanted to see them. I wanted *them* to see *me*.

Finally Harmony sighed. "If you insist on going, we can't stop you. All we can do is warn you. Going back will not be what you expect. Things won't go any better for you than they did for me."

I thought about her story. She had traveled a much greater distance, and at a time when travel was much more difficult. She had left with no plan to return, but I would have a plan.

"Two days to get there, one day to say my good-byes, and two days to get back," I told them. "I'll be gone for five days, that's all."

"A lot can happen in five days," said Aaron, but there was a sad resignation in his voice, because he knew I had made up my mind.

I planned to go on foot, but Aaron, as opposed as he was to it, had a better idea.

"If you go on foot, you could freeze to death. We don't have any clothes here warm enough to see you over the mountains. It's best if the monks take you."

"But don't they serve Abuelo? They'll never do it!"

He gave me a halfhearted grin. "The monks won't ever know they're taking you."

He explained how, once a week, a group of monks arrived on a hillside to the east to deliver supplies and take away the garbage that could not be composted.

On this particular week, I would be part of the garbage.

Harmony went to visit Abuelo that morning, to make sure he was distracted and his eyes weren't on the hillside as Aaron and I climbed out of the southern tip of the valley. I took off my gossamer gown and dressed in something more "earthly" for my journey, and Aaron brought along a burlap sack. Anyone who saw us making our way up the hillside would think we were just taking out the garbage.

This spot to the east and high up the hillside was the only place where mountains didn't rise too high to climb. Grass still grew there, but it wasn't as lush and green as it was lower in the valley. This grass had turned yellow, and spots were turning brown. As I looked back into the valley, I could see a thin rim of yellow grass that circled the entire valley of De León. I had never noticed it before. Aaron knelt down and rubbed his hands across the yellow grass, a look of worry on his face.

"This is a bad idea," he told me, in a last-ditch effort to change my mind. "No one in Flock's Rest deserves your good-byes."

"Wouldn't you have wanted to say good-bye to your parents?" I asked him.

"No," he said—but I could tell he wasn't sure if he meant it.

At the crest of the hill were a dozen sacks, like the one Aaron carried, all filled with the trash of De León.

"Five days," Aaron reminded me. "That's all you get." He opened his sack to show me that sewn to the inside were furry animal skins that, unfortunately, still had some of the animal attached. "I know it's not pretty," he said, "but it's the best I could do on such short notice. It'll keep you warm for the journey." It didn't look all that different from the bag of roadkill I had once carried out from my room.

"Thank you," I told him. It was all I could do not to lose my breakfast.

"You should wear a heavy winter coat when you come back," he told me. Then, looking around to make sure no one had followed us up, he gave me instructions for my return. "Be careful that no one from the outside world sees you. Come the way you did the first time—follow the path behind the old billboard."

"How far?" I asked. The night of my arrival had been such a blur, and I had passed out by the time the monks had found me. I had no idea how far De León was from civilization.

"Twenty miles," he said. "But it feels like a lot more because it's almost all mountains. As you get closer, you'll see the monastery on top of a hill, but whatever you do, don't go near it, because the monks won't know you're one of us if they see you. It's their duty to make sure no one from the outside ever finds us, and they take their job very seriously, if you know what I mean."

I nodded. These so-called monks sounded more like ninjas, but I kept my opinion to myself.

"Turn west at your first glimpse of the monastery," Aaron continued. "There's no path after that, but if you follow the setting sun, you'll come to De León. Good luck."

He hugged me tightly, like he had changed his mind and wasn't going to let me get into the sack.

"I'll be back before you know it. I promise."

"I don't think I'll sleep until you are."

I gave him a kiss that wasn't long enough for either of us, then I stepped into the fur-lined bag. Aaron covered me with trash, just in case the monks looked inside, then he tied the sack closed.

Only after I was tied into the bag and I couldn't see him did I hear him say: "I love you, Cara."

And then he was gone.

After he left, I sat there for hours, waiting for the monks to arrive, afraid to move the slightest bit in case they might be close enough to see. As I waited, I kept playing in my mind the last thing Harmony had said to me before she had hugged me good-bye and hurried off to Abuelo's that morning.

"Do not linger in the outside world," she had warned me. "Say your final good-byes quickly, and come home to us."

"What will happen if I stay too long?" I had asked. "Will I turn ugly again?"

"I don't know," Harmony had answered. "But I do know there are worse things than being ugly."

PART THREE

▲

"CYGNUS FATALIS"

18
▲
return TO THE FLOCK

Traveling as garbage was not a highlight of my life, but some-times you do what you have to do. The monks never knew I was there. I suppose I wasn't much heavier than what they were used to hauling. The fur around me kept me warm, but not warm enough. I shivered most of the way, and wondered if I would die of hypothermia and end up as part of the garbage after all. *Trashes-to-ashes,* I thought. It almost made me giggle, which, under the circumstances, would have been disastrous. The jour-ney took a day and a half, and although they rested, I barely slept. I was hungry and, even more, thirsty. It was unbearable. Finally, toward the end of the second day, my bag was hurled into a hard, rough place, where I landed with a bruising crunch.

I let the pain peak, then fade, clenching my teeth so that I didn't make a sound. Then, when I was sure they were gone, I pulled myself out of the bag.

I was in a Dumpster. I stood up to get my bearings. I was out behind a gas station, and it was after dark. It was chilly, but nowhere near as cold as it had been in the higher altitudes as we crossed the mountains.

I climbed out and walked around to the front of the station, trying to stretch my cramped arms and legs. The second the gas-station attendant saw me, he swaggered over to me.

"Hey, little lady," he said. He was just a couple of years older than me, nineteen at the most. "What can I do you for?"

He was all goggly-eyed, and it took me a moment to realize he didn't see the Flock's Rest Monster when he looked at me. He saw someone beautiful. It amazed me that he didn't seem to notice I was covered in garbage.

"Which way to Flock's Rest?" I asked.

"No easy way to get there from here," he said. "That's clear over the mountains. The nearest road that crosses over is twenty-five miles away."

So the monks had taken me in the other direction. Well, that was just a minor inconvenience. I could still get there, and make it back, in time.

He smiled at me, showing me a cracked tooth, and tried to act all charming. "I get off in a couple of hours. I could give you a ride if you like. I know where it is; I was just there 'bout a month ago."

Something told me it wouldn't be a good idea. "No thanks," I told him, and he seemed a little hurt.

"Hey, I understand," he said. "A pretty girl like you—why would you take a ride from a guy like me? Right? 'Cept, of course, I got a really good car. Tiger-skin seats." He winked at me, and I rolled my eyes. Is this what pretty girls had to put up with all the time? "Runs like a dream," he said. "Just got it last month down at DeFido's. That's how come I know Flock's Rest."

I laughed at that. "If you got your car at DeFido's, then you got ripped off," I told him. "Trust me, I know. He's my father."

Suddenly he started snapping his fingers like something was

wrong with him. "You—you—you're that missing DeFido girl. Holy Mother of—no friggin' way! I gots to call the cops, that's what I gots to do."

"No," I said. "No, don't!"

But he wasn't listening. "Oh yeah, they got a reward out for you."

"My parents offered a reward?"

I was actually impressed, until he said, "Five hundred dollars. Get myself some spinners for my car."

Five hundred bucks, I thought. Is that what I was worth to them? I knew people who offered higher rewards for their lost cats.

He ran into the gas-station office, and I ran after him. "No, stop," I said. He was already picking up the phone, but then he stopped when he looked at the "Missing" poster taped right there on his window. It didn't have a picture of me, because there were no pictures. Instead there was a police sketch. It was ugly, it was awful. It was me. Or at least the *old* me.

"Hey, hold on. This ain't you."

He looked to the poster, then to me, then to the poster again.

"No, you're right," I said, thinking quickly. "That's my sister. My sister's the one who's missing. Not me."

He looked at me, the expression on his face souring. "I guess there's no reward for you, is there?"

I shook my head. "No. Sorry." And I hurried out before he could offer me a ride again.

Five days, I thought as I walked down the road, and two already gone. Not much I could accomplish in what little time I had. But I didn't need to accomplish anything, did I? All I had to do was have a nice long sit-down with Mom and Dad. Maybe pack a bag of what few things I cared about, and leave forever. If I had time, maybe I'd go out to Vista View, find Miss Leticia's grave, and pay my respects.

The gas station was on a lonely road, with only a few homes nearby. I changed out of my garbage-covered clothes in someone's toolshed, took a long drink from the yard hose, then hosed myself off with its freezing water, and took some clothes that were hanging out to dry in the backyard. Then I started walking.

About five miles down the road, my feet were hurting something awful, and although a number of folks stopped to offer me a ride, I didn't take them up on it—mainly because they were all guys of varying ages, with their tongues practically hanging out like wolves when they looked at me. That wasn't the kind of attention I wanted from strangers, and I wasn't foolish enough to get into a car with any of them. It was a different world for me now. I had to get used to that.

Finally, a family in a minivan pulled up next to me.

"Honey, are you all right?" the woman asked, leaning out of the passenger-side window. "You know, it's dangerous to be on the road like this after dark. You might get hit by a car. Would you like a ride somewhere?"

This was a ride I felt safe taking, so I smiled, thanked them, and hopped in.

I sat in the back with the kids. A little boy no older than six, sucking on some sticky candy that made his lips blue, smiled at me. "You're pretty," he said.

And I laughed, because it was true!

Flock's Rest wasn't exactly on their way, but they didn't have the heart to leave me by the side of the road somewhere. That's another thing about being beautiful: People go out of their way to help you. It was almost midnight when they reached Flock's Rest. I had them drop me at the entrance to my trailer park.

Dad would be sitting with a beer, watching RetroToob and dreaming of his lost youth. Momma would probably still be up reading. Vance would be asleep, if he hadn't had too much pop at dinner.

As excited as I was, I was scared, too. My father always said, "You can't make a Ford a Ferrari," and yet here I was, all shiny and new. Cara: the sports model. I could give them no explanation for the change I had gone through. I couldn't tell them where I'd been, or about the water of the fountain, no matter how much they asked.

I knocked on the door. No answer at first, so I knocked again. Finally, Momma answered it and looked at me, squinting her eyes.

"Hi," I said.

She wasn't shocked. She didn't even seem surprised. She just seemed a little put out over answering the door in her robe at midnight. "Can I help you?" she said.

I stood there for a moment, dumbfounded. She had no idea who I was.

"Momma, it's me."

She looked at me blankly, her mind trying to mesh what she saw with what she knew.

Then she backed up and went kind of white.

"Franklin," she said, her voice all wavery. "Franklin, come quick."

Few things would lift my dad off the couch once he had settled in. But that tone of voice did the trick. As he came to her, I stepped inside. Now Vance was standing at his bedroom door, half-awake, wondering what was going on.

"It's me," I said. "It's Cara." And then, just for effect, I flicked my hair the way models do. "Don't you recognize me?"

Just silence for the longest time.

Vance was the first to react. "No. Way."

"Honey?" Dad said in the same wavery voice that Mom had.

And then it was like whatever was holding them back just fell away. Momma rushed at me and took me in her arms.

"My baby, my baby," she cried.

Even Dad cried. "We thought you ran away," he said. "Or worse."

"I did," I told them. "But it's okay now."

While Momma and Dad were still hugging me, Vance came over and looked me up and down. "What happened to you?"

And then, to my surprise, Momma turned to him, grabbed him by the shoulders, and looked at him sternly. "Don't you ask that! I'm sure Cara will tell us in her own time, won't you, honey?"

I nodded, knowing that I wouldn't. Maybe Momma sensed that, because she said, "Besides, true miracles don't always have explanations. Otherwise they wouldn't be miracles."

Vance looked down. "Yes, ma'am."

I told them I was only back for a little while—that people were waiting for me.

"I understand," Momma said, even though we both knew she didn't.

We all hugged and hugged. Momma whispered things you whisper to babies, and when all the hugging was done, I went to my room.

I thought they would have changed it in the months that I had been gone. I figured they'd turn it into a reading room, or a sewing room, or something. Make the memory of me go away. But they hadn't. It was just as I had left it. I even found the little "find the answers" note—a reminder that the answers had been found, and were waiting for me back in De León. Back *home*.

Before going to bed, though, I went up to my dresser and, for one final time, played my old familiar game. Would Cara do it today? Was today the day she would win? Without the slightest hesitation, I grabbed the sheet that covered the mirror and pulled it down. No more mourning in this house! At last I looked at myself in my own mirror. As far as I was concerned, I could have looked forever.

The next morning, we ate our family breakfast like usual, but there was a certain air of terror all around the table, because miracles are frightening things. No matter how much Momma wanted to follow a don't-ask-don't-tell policy with regard to my metamorphosis, it demanded some explanation. Dad began to delicately ask about it. It was like playing a game of twenty questions around a time bomb.

"Was it something . . . surgical?" Dad asked, without looking up at me.

"Not really," I said.

"Herbal, then? They're making amazing strides in vitamin therapy these days."

That was actually closer to the truth. I wondered if the fountain could be considered an herbal treatment.

"Vitamin therapy doesn't straighten teeth," Momma said. "That takes some sort of . . . *intervention.*"

"So we're back to miracles again," said Dad, a bit frustrated.

No one said anything for a bit, and then Vance mumbled, "I think maybe Cara made a pact with the devil."

Momma brought down her fork so hard it cracked her plate in half.

"Sorry," Vance said. Momma didn't scold him. Maybe because she secretly felt it was in the realm of possibility.

"Actually," I said, with a completely straight face, "I was abducted by aliens."

Stunned silence from everyone . . . until I couldn't hold it anymore and cracked a smile. Vance was the first to laugh, then Dad, then Mom, and before long, we were all engulfed in a giggle fit that lasted at least three or four minutes. After that, they stopped asking.

I finished my breakfast quickly and asked if Momma could take me to school early. If I was going to accomplish anything during my single day in Flock's Rest, I'd have to use the time wisely—and the more I thought about it, the more things I realized I wanted to do . . . because this wasn't just about saying good-bye. This was also about saying "good riddance."

19

▲

THE new GIRL

Momma brought me to school and told the office staff I was her niece, Linda. I might be moving into town, she said, and could they be darlings and let me sit in on class while I was visiting? She sold them on me like my dad sold a car—not a word of truth, and bought for the highest price possible. I didn't mind being Linda DeFido for a day. After all, Linda was my middle name.

There was still plenty of time before the bell rang, so I went out into the yard to size up what had changed since I had left. As I suspected, nothing had changed. The same kids in the same groups. Of course, some girls were hanging on different boys' shoulders, but even then, the shoulders on which they hung were the predictable ones. One couple, however, had stood the test of time. Marshall and Marisol. They were all slithered around each other in the yard, like always. I made a beeline straight toward them.

"Excuse me," I said innocently, getting their attention.

I had Marshall's eye immediately. Marisol already looked worried.

"Aren't you Marshall Astor, of the famous Astors?"

Marisol answered for him. "That's none of your business. Who are you?"

"Oh, I'm sorry," I said, as sweetly as could be. "I'm Linda DeFido. I'll be moving here from Billington." I kept my eye on Marshall, totally ignoring Marisol. "I remember you from one of last year's football games. I have never seen a run that long. I remember wishing that you were on our team."

Marshall just smiled dumbly. I made sure I had a lock on his eyes like a tractor beam. "So you're moving here?" he asked.

"*And* she's a DeFido?" said Marisol. "That family is a bunch of losers."

"Oh, we're all right," I said, still smiling. "Except, of course, for my poor cousin, Cara—wherever she is."

Marshall broke eye contact and looked down. "The DeFidos don't like me much. They think I'm the reason their daughter ran off. Your cousin, I mean."

"Oh, they don't think that," I said. "They know that Cara brought it on herself. They don't blame you at all."

Marshall smiled. "Really?"

"You should come by and talk to my uncle. I'm sure he'll be very forgiving."

"Yeah," he said, still smiling. "Maybe I'll do that."

"You will not," said Marisol. "You don't need to talk to trailer trash."

"Not all trash lives in trailers," I told her. She started going colors I didn't know the human face could go. "What's the matter, Marisol?" I asked. "You didn't choke on your gum, did you?"

"How'd you know my name?"

"Oh," I said, "you've got a reputation. Even as far as Billington."

"What?" Her mouth opened, and she just looked at me, her head shaking slightly, like her pea brain had just popped its one blood vessel.

Marshall looked at her like she was suddenly something unclean, and I went on my merry way. This was the start of a wonderful day!

I was the center of attention in every class, and when I walked into the lunchroom, all heads turned, boys and girls alike. They were whispering about me. By force of habit, I looked for my usual empty table—but without the old Cara here, creating her aura of untouchability, there were no empty tables.

I thought I'd find Marshall and Marisol again, and play with their meager minds some more—but then I spotted Gerardo.

I'd known I would see him today, and I thought I'd be okay with it—that I was beyond all those mixed-up feelings I had for him—but I was wrong. It only took a moment for all the feelings to come back.

It didn't make sense to me—I had Aaron now, didn't I? Gerardo was a flyspeck compared to Aaron, and yet he made me numb and light-headed in a way that Aaron never quite did. It made me mad, but not mad enough to turn and walk the other way.

I went to the table where he sat with his friends—and let me tell you, they made a space for me like I was Moses and they were the Red Sea.

"You need a place to sit?"

"Sit here!"

"No, sit here, he smells!"

"I've got lots of room for you on the end!"

"Don't listen to those idiots, you can sit wherever you want. As long as it's next to me!"

I smiled, and didn't accept any of their invitations. I knew just how to play this. "Someone told me one of you boys knows something about computers?"

And all of a sudden all five boys at the table were computer experts. I knew for a fact at least three of them weren't, but that didn't stop them from practically climbing all over one another to impress me with their know-how.

I didn't know all that much about computers, but I knew enough to be able to weed out the poseurs.

"Good," I said, "because I need to find a way to install a thirty-two-bit sound card in a sixteen-bit slot."

Sudden silence from four of the five. But Gerardo perked up.

"It sounds like you need to upgrade your motherboard. I could do that for you."

I put out my hand and smiled at him.

"Hi, I'm Linda."

"Gerardo," he said, shaking my hand. "I was a friend of your cousin's."

For a second it caught me by surprise. Then I realized, in a high school, news traveled at the speed of pheromones. Probably every boy in school heard that I was a DeFido. Of course, they didn't know *which* DeFido I was.

"Gerardo . . ." I said, pretending to think about his name. "I think Cara talked about you."

"She did?"

"She was in love with him," said one of the other boys.

Gerardo shrugged. "We were just friends."

"Yeah, that's what she said. She said you were dating Nikki somebody."

"Ah," said Gerardo, "that was months ago."

I looked down at my plate, then picked up my brownie and put it on Gerardo's plate, like I used to do back in the ugly days.

He looked a little creeped out for a second. "Just how much did Cara talk about me?"

I didn't answer him; I just gave him a wink. "Have a nice lunch." Then I stood up and left with the grace of a swan.

There's this expression. I think it's French. *Femme fatale.* It means "deadly woman," but really means more than that. It means a woman so beautiful, she can twist the world around her finger.

That was me now, and until today, I had no idea how much fun twisting could be. The problem was, I only had today to do it, and it frustrated me. I wanted to take on this school like a tornado, and leave people quivering in my wake—but with only one day, I'd be little more than a passing breeze. I was already trying to figure ways to stretch out my visit—if only for a few more hours.

I knew Marisol had started spreading nasty rumors about me. Marshall was already preening to get my attention, and when I waved to Gerardo in the hall a little bit later in the day, he walked right into a locker. Femme fatale. In a way, it was so much more satisfying than just being one of the beautiful people in De León.

By the end of the day, Marshall had already asked me on a date, and I'd accepted—mainly because I knew once Marisol found out, she'd gnaw her own limbs off. Unfortunately, the date was for Saturday, so I wouldn't be able to follow through. It burned me that Marisol would have the satisfaction of my permanent disappearance.

Gerardo wasted no time, either. He showed up at my house right after school.

"Hi, is Linda home?"

"Who?" said my idiot brother, who had answered the door. "Oh. Linda, right. Yeah, she's here."

I ducked into my room and tried to get the sudden flush to leave my face. I didn't even think he knew where I lived. When I stepped out, I had the poise and presence of a movie star.

"Gerardo," I said. "How nice to see you!"

"Hi. I came over to fix that computer problem you were having."

"Excuse me?"

He held up a bag of cables and components. "Your motherboard?"

"Oh. Oh, right." The thing is, I didn't even have a computer. "Well, that's all right. We sent it to the shop already. But thank you."

He looked disappointed. "Oh. Okay. Well. Bye."

He turned to leave, but I put my hand on his shoulder and stopped him.

"Would you like a drink?" I said.

He smiled. "Sure."

I figure he would have said "sure" to whatever I offered him. He wanted to stay as much as I wanted him to.

I got him some pop from the fridge. We sat there for a long

time, just sipping, and trying to burp up the bubbles quietly enough so the other wouldn't hear.

"So," he finally said.

"So," I said back to him.

He looked at me and looked away, then looked back at me again. "Why don't you give me your number? Maybe I'll call you or something."

"My cell phone, you mean? I don't have one."

"Okay, then give me your home number."

I thought it was an odd request because he already knew the number here. But then, maybe by asking for my number he was testing the waters, to see where he stood. If I gave him the number, it meant it was all right for him to call me—and that was one step short of asking me out. I wished he would have done it right then and there, but when it came to girls, I guess Gerardo wasn't quite as pushy as Marshall. I smiled at him, grabbed a pen and paper from the counter, happily wrote down the number, and handed it to him.

He looked at it closely. "Hmm. Right." Then folded it and put it in his pocket. "Well, see you in school, Linda."

He left, and the second he was gone, I went into my room and did a little victory dance. And then I remembered, if he did work up enough nerve to call me for a date, I wouldn't be here. I'd be back in De León. I flopped on my bed, cursing the unfairness of it all. If I could have just one date with Gerardo, just one, I could leave this place forever and be happy, couldn't I? But that wasn't going to happen.

That night, as I tossed and turned in bed, a war began in my mind. On one side were Aaron and Harmony and Abuelo—all the people of De León. I was truly one of them. I felt accepted, I belonged—I truly did miss Aaron—and besides, I had made him a promise that I'd be back in five days.

But there was that other side. The side that said, *What's a few more days gonna hurt? Finish what you started. Get your revenge on Marshall and Marisol. Have that one night out with Gerardo. Twist them all around your finger until you're satisfied. And then you can go back to De León forever.*

The war raged inside me, and with the hours counting down until I had to leave to meet my deadline, I had no idea which side was going to win.

I woke up the next morning and found myself standing in the corner, facing northwest. I had sleepwalked again. I was still drawn to De León. It was time to say that final good-bye and begin my journey back.

When I turned around, I saw Vance standing at my door, watching me. He didn't wisecrack, he just watched me. He seemed almost afraid to come in.

"The place you went," he said. "It's in that direction, isn't it?"

I nodded. First I was pleased that he had figured it out, then I got worried.

"You won't tell anyone, will you?"

He didn't answer me. "Are you going back?"

"Yes," I told him.

"Good."

Then he walked off. He would never understand—and neither would anyone else. That's why I had to get back to De León.

But did I have to leave right then? I could stay for part of the day, couldn't I? If I left after school, and came home to say good-bye, I could get a ride to the old billboard before dark. If I had a bright enough flashlight, I could walk through the night and shorten the two-day trek a bit. I still might be a little bit late in getting back to De León, but at least I'd get there.

I looked at the mirror above my dresser, studying my face. Right away I could see that I wasn't a hundred percent this morning. It was just bed hair, and the kind of droopy eyes and dark circles you have when you first wake up—but ever since washing in the fountain, I had never had messy hair or droopy eyes in the morning. I always woke up like they do on TV—looking perfect. It wasn't a big deal at all, but it bothered me . . . so I took a deep breath and shook my head so that my hair flung to the left and right.

And the strangest thing happened. My hair fell into perfect place—the rings under my eyes faded—and I swear to you, for the briefest instant, it was as if the sunlight in the room dimmed, and the colors on the wallpaper faded just the tiniest bit.

I decided it was just my imagination, but deep down, I knew that it wasn't.

The big news at school was that Marshall and Marisol had broken up last night. From what I heard, Marshall just couldn't keep himself from bragging about our upcoming date to his friends. It got back to Marisol. Word was they had a breakup so vicious, somebody should have called Animal Control. It happened at the bowling alley. Marisol confronted him, so he accused her of sneaking around with other boys. She chased him down lane twelve with a bowling ball, he slipped, went flying into the pins, and got himself a strike. Now he had a bruise on his forehead from where the automatic pinsetter kept coming down, trying to pick him up.

That should have been all the victory I needed, but I was now like a shark after smelling blood.

Marisol followed me before class started. She was trying to keep me from seeing her, but I knew she was there, so when the bell rang, I ducked into the girls' bathroom, knowing she would follow. Let her think she had cornered me.

Sure enough, she came in about ten seconds later. It was just the two of us in there, and Marisol had a look in her eyes that was as murderous as any I'd ever seen.

"Good morning, Marisol," I said brightly. "Having yourself a good day?"

Her hair was unkempt, a little straggly, like she hadn't been using her salon-approved conditioner. I guess she had more things to worry about now than just her hair.

"You listen and you listen good," said Marisol. "I know you are not who you say you are, 'cause I've been checking with folks I know, and there's no Linda DeFido from Billington High."

I calmly dipped my hands under the faucet and washed my face. Was that a zit I saw trying to come through on my left cheek? No—it couldn't be.

"You're right, Marisol," I told her.

"So you had better tell me who you really are."

I smiled and took my time. "Don't you know? I'm the girl who just stole away your boyfriend and made a fool out of you. Your reign as the queen of Flock's Rest High is over."

Then the fury in Marisol's eyes took a strange turn. "You

know," she said, "we don't have to be enemies." It was the same expression she had on that day in seventh grade when she had asked me to take the fall for her cheating ways. "People don't understand girls like us," Marisol said. "Not really. Why spend all our time tearing each other down when we could share everything?"

"I don't share anything with you, and I never will." I started to move toward her slowly, and she backed away until she hit the tile wall. She was still angry, yes, but fear was taking over.

"You still don't recognize me, do you? Maybe because you never really looked at me."

"I don't understand," said Marisol.

"You don't? Well, let me spell it out for you. *G-R-O-T-E-S-Q-U-E.*"

And I saw in her eyes the moment she figured it out.

"No! It's impossible . . . Cara?"

Her face began to stretch in horror and disbelief. I took another step closer.

"*A-B-O-M-I-N-A-B-L-E.*"

She couldn't speak now. Her throat had closed up; she could barely breathe.

I grabbed her by her pretty little sweater, pushing her hard against the wall. And that's when things, as strange as they were, went to a whole new level, as I spelled one more word for her, looking her dead in the eyes.

"*M—*"

The color of her eyes went from bright blue to a muddy gray.

"*O—*"

Acne began to rupture forth from her skin like the earth pushing up mountains.

"N—"

Her earlobes drooped, and one whole ear started to sink lower than the other.

"S—"

Her strawberry blond hair with the pretty highlights lost its sheen and started to tangle.

"T—"

Her pouty little lips drooped and cracked.

"E—"

Her teeth began to fade to a sickly shade of gray.

"R!"

I let go of her, and stepped back to look at her transformation. I should have been horrified, but all I could feel was satisfaction as deep as the Caldero cavern.

"My, my, Marisol—you're as ugly as . . . roadkill!"

Marisol reached up, feeling the change as she touched her face, and she screamed. "What did you do?" she wailed. "What did you do to me?!" Even her voice had changed. It was the raspy screech of a hag.

She caught her reflection in the mirror, but only for an instant before the mirror shattered. Then she ran into a stall to hide, sobbing, as if it was the end of the world.

I stepped gently over the broken glass, feeling it crackle beneath the soles of my shoes, and I picked up a mirror shard from the ground, catching a bit of my own reflection in it.

There was no zit on my cheek—not even a red spot. I must have been wrong. My complexion was creamy pure.

I was filled with absolute contentment as I strode out of that restroom. That was the moment I knew that I wasn't going back to

De León. Not tonight, not tomorrow, or the next day, or the next. No matter what I had promised—no matter how much I would miss Aaron, what I had now in Flock's Rest was worth the cost.

Harmony had been wrong. She said there would be no place for me in my old life, but I now knew otherwise. In De León, I was one face in a crowd of beautiful people, but here I was the star. And I was going to enjoy it.

20

▲

UGLIFICATIONS

ometimes you make decisions that you know are wrong, but you make them anyway. When you're a little kid you think, *Should I hit my brother and make him cry, even though I know I'm going to get in trouble for it?* But the force of your will wrestles down the sense in your head and you do it anyway.

When you get older, the situations aren't quite as simple, and although you tend to have more sense, you tend to be more willful as well. Sometimes that sense wins out, and other times you set yourself up for a world of suffering.

My parents seemed happy that I had chosen to stay, although I think they, like Vance, would have been relieved if I didn't. It wasn't so hard making the transition to being Linda DeFido. My father knew a guy who knew a guy who could make all the computers in the world believe you were Marilyn Monroe, if that's what you wanted. He even managed to get fictional records transferred over from Billington High, with grades not quite as high as my real ones. Like that mattered now.

As for what happened to Marisol, I didn't understand at the time how I had "uglified" her. I thought that maybe it was like Miss Leticia had once said: Spells and spelling weren't all that different—maybe I had a little bit of witch in me after all. Maybe the fountain had brought it out.

She stayed in that bathroom stall all day long. The counselor couldn't get her out. The principal couldn't get her out. In the end, her parents came and her daddy kicked the door open.

I wasn't there to see the commotion when they saw what she looked like. All I know is they rushed her off to the hospital. The rumor was that she had come down with some rare disfiguring disease, like acute leprosy or something.

I had my date with Marshall that Saturday. He talked about himself, bragging mostly. I made up stuff about my fictional life as Linda DeFido.

He walked me home, his arm around my shoulder.

"I'd like to spend more time with you," he said. "Marisol wasn't right for me. I mean, I feel bad about her getting sick and all, but, hey, I've got my own life, right?"

He smiled at me. There was a gentle look in his eyes. Was Marshall Astor falling in love with me? I wondered. How deeply would he have to fall until I could effectively break his heart? I thought about that painful night at the homecoming dance. True, a lot of what had happened was my own fault, but I still couldn't wait to make him feel as miserable as I had felt when I ran out that night. Maybe then he'd have a glimpse of what it had been like to be me.

"Sure, Marshall," I said, gently rubbing his arm. "I'd like to see you again."

The moment became awkward, and he looked off—and pointed at the window boxes. The ones that held my mom's marigolds.

"Someone oughta water those," he said.

I looked at them. They had completely lost their petals. They were all stem and seedpod—twisted leggy things with little round black heads.

"I guess everything around here can't be as beautiful as you," Marshall said. Then he left me at my front door with a kiss that didn't make him puke.

"Was that Marshall Astor?" Momma asked as I stepped in.

"Yes. And Dad didn't even have to give him a free car to go out with me."

Dad grumbled from his spot on the sofa.

"First that boy Gerardo . . . and now Marshall," Momma said. "Exactly which one are you dating?"

"Both of them," I told her. "Any of them. *All* of them." And why not? I could date as many boys as I wanted. I'd earned that right. And if me seeing Marshall would make Gerardo jealous, all the better.

"Oh, by the way," I told Momma, "you need to replace your marigolds."

She wrinkled her brows. "Replace them? Why? They were fine this morning."

Gerardo never called me. Even though he had my number— even though I made it clear that I wanted him to call, he never did. It was just plain frustrating. Marshall asked me out again, though—and so I agreed to go to the movies with him, if for no other reason than to spite Gerardo.

At the movie, Marshall held me a little too close, tried to go a little too far, and I slapped him a little too hard. After that, he acted like a scolded puppy for the rest of the night.

He left me at my door, I let him give me a good night kiss, and I accepted his apologies graciously. I didn't tell him that his weren't the kisses I wanted.

There was something different about Marshall now. Maybe it was just that I was seeing through new eyes, but he didn't seem quite as good-looking to me anymore.

It wasn't just him, either. I found imperfections in everything and everybody at school. This boy had bad breath, that girl had bad hair, this one's fat, and that one's got an odd-shaped head. Was it just my imagination, or were all those things getting a little bit worse each day?

I even saw it in my family. Since when did Vance's eyes look so beady, and his two front teeth look so big? Since when did Dad's cheeks look so sunken in? And Momma's hair—had it always been so thin?

People didn't change like that, I told myself. It was all in my head. Could it be that I was surrounded by so much beauty in De León that the rest of the world paled by comparison?

I went out with Marshall four more times, making sure I controlled how far things went on every date. Then, after the last one, I heard the words that every girl longs to hear.

"I love you, Linda," Marshall said, and I knew that he meant it. I don't know if he had ever even said that to Marisol.

I broke up with him the next day without explanation. He was devastated.

Now, with Marisol and Marshall taken care of, I turned my attentions to Gerardo. I thought that maybe he was keeping his distance, thinking I was really interested in Marshall. I made it clear around school that I was now available, and although every other boy in school began fighting to carry my books or sit with me at lunch, Gerardo wasn't one of them.

There were times I caught him watching me, though. During classes we had together, he would steal a peek, then look the other way and not look at me again for the rest of the period. I would squeeze my way into his lunch table, and within a minute, he would excuse himself and go sit somewhere else. Winning him over should have been easy, but now I realized this was trickier than vengeance.

When I started finding love letters shoved into the vent of my locker, I thought for sure they were from Gerardo—that he had finally come around. But no, those letters were all from Marshall, professing his undying love, hoping beyond hope to win me back. I sent his letters back to him with his spelling corrected.

Most popular. Most attractive. Most desirable. I was all of those things, but it simply wasn't enough. Well, if I could strip Marisol of her beauty, then I could strip Gerardo of his resistance. I knew I could!

I caught up with him one day after school walking home, and I matched his pace, even though he was trying to walk faster.

"I thought you were going to call me."

"What for?" he said. "It looks like you've got all the boys you can handle."

I shrugged. "I'm still waiting for the right one."

"Well, good luck finding him."

He took a shortcut through a weedy yard and into an alley. I followed. "You've been avoiding me, and you know it," I told him. "I just want to know why."

"Because I don't think you're good for me," he said. "In fact, I don't think you're good for anyone." That was Gerardo, all right. Always honest.

"I don't know what you mean."

"Yeah, you do. You toyed with Marshall, and now he's even more of a blithering idiot than he was before. You did something to Marisol, too, didn't you? I can't prove it, and I don't know what it was you did—but you did something that's keeping her out of school."

"Gerardo," I said, still forcing sweetness into my voice, "you make me sound like a monster."

"Yeah," he said, "the Flock's Rest Monster."

I pursed my lips, keeping my mouth shut. He looked at me then, for the first time in our whole conversation.

"Yeah, I know who you are, Cara. Maybe no one else does, but I do, so you can drop the act."

At first I was going to deny it—but what good would that have done? I took a deep breath and let it out. "When did you find out?"

He reached into his pocket and pulled out a little slip of paper, handing it to me. It was the phone number I had written down for him on my first day back. Like an idiot, I had written "Cara" instead of "Linda."

"At first I didn't believe it," Gerardo said. "But the more I watched you, the more I realized who you were. You knew too many things about too many people."

Okay, I thought, it was time to change strategies now. No more deceit. It was time for honesty. "I can tell you how it happened—how I changed."

"I don't want to know." He hitched his backpack higher on

his shoulder and picked up his pace again. "Everything about you scares me, Cara. The way you look, the way you act . . ." I wasn't expecting to hear that—not from him. "You got yourself a whole school to play with," he told me. "So go find yourself a guy who can only see your face, and not the rest."

"Why are you treating me like this? I'm still the same person I was before."

He shook his head. "No, you're not. You were just ugly on the outside before. But your inside and outside kind of switched places, didn't they?"

His words were like a brutal slap. I wanted to strike back, but I held my temper because I knew it would chase him away. Instead I turned on my newfound charm. "You could be dating the most beautiful girl in Flock's Rest," I said to him. "Doesn't that mean anything to you?"

"How long before you spit me out like you spat out Marshall?"

"You're not Marshall," I told him. "I would *never* do that to you."

Suddenly I heard a twang of metal, and Gerardo's lip began to bleed.

He put his hand up to his lip and took it away, seeing the blood on his fingers. The blood had now spread across his braces. The wire on his top teeth had sprung and was sticking out at a weird angle. One of those teeth was turned funny. Just one—like it had fought so powerfully against the wire trying to hold it in place that the wire busted.

With his hand held to his mouth, he said, "You see, Cara? Nothing good happens when you're around."

And he hurried across the street to get away from me.

What does it take to turn a heart black? One too many cruel tricks? One too many rejections? Or maybe it's something we do to ourselves. Evil people never think of themselves as evil. Maybe because they still remember themselves as good—or perhaps they see a future self resting peacefully in a time and place of goodness. A place where they can repent for all the awful things they did to get there.

I can't say exactly where I was, or what I was on the inside. All I knew was that I was stunning to the eye, and it blinded me to so many things. After that day, I took to brooding about Gerardo, the way that Marshall brooded about me, and feeling more and more miserable about how things had turned out. I didn't notice that fewer and fewer boys were wanting to sit with me at lunch, and that fewer and fewer girls wanted to talk with me after school. I did start to notice other things, though.

Flock's Rest had never been the most beautiful town in the world, but it wasn't an eyesore, either. Or at least I had never seen it that way. Just as with people, I was seeing our town through completely different eyes. Eyes that had known the simple, perfect beauty of De León.

I had been home for about six weeks when I really became aware of it. Driving in the car with Momma one day, I spent some time looking—*really* looking at the state of our town. Lawns were patchy and yellow, and the paint on the houses wasn't just peeling, it was fading like someone had come in the middle of the night and robbed the color. The houses themselves had a weariness to them. Their windows looked like old eyes.

Their porches seemed like mouths hung open in exhaustion. Every building in town sagged under its own weight, as if it was just longing to crumble to the ground.

"Momma," I asked, "has Flock's Rest always looked this bad?"

"Well, honey," she said, "a town gets old."

It was more than that, though. I pointed out a garden we passed. "Just look at that!" I remembered that garden—it used to be all full of rosebushes, but now it was half-dead, and the few hardy plants still alive looked like the weeds that pop up in a highway divider.

Momma shrugged. "It's just the time of year, dear. Even though we're not in a snow zone, not all that many things grow in the winter. And besides, maybe the owner likes it growing wild."

I would have argued, but just then we hit a pothole that nearly ejected me from the car and completely rattled my thoughts. Seemed to me there were more ruined roads in town, too.

I looked at the barren gray streets and sad, sallow faces around me, day after day, and I began to long once more for that place of color and light. That valley more beautiful than a painting. Because I might have been the queen of Flock's Rest, but I couldn't imagine a life where there was no beauty to see except for my own reflection.

On Valentine's Day, I walked home from school alone, just as I had in the days when I was ugly. I had begun to feel sick halfway through school that day, but I had become so good at denial, I told myself it was nothing and believed it.

When I came through the gate of our trailer park, I had to do a quick double take to make sure I was in the right place. Our park, which wasn't too attractive a place to begin with, had fallen into the realm of utter squalor. The lawn blight sweeping through town seemed to have begun here. It had killed much of the grass, but no one cared. They were as untroubled as my mother was with her window boxes, which now grew nothing but mildew and toadstools.

When I stepped inside the door, Momma was standing there, holding the phone and looking a bit ill herself.

"Yes," she said. "I understand. Our prayers will be with them."

"Prayers?" I asked. "Who are we praying for?"

"Sit down, honey."

It's never a good thing when one of your parents tells you to sit down. Especially in that deeply understanding tone of voice. I did as I was told.

"I'm afraid something awful has happened," Momma told me. Then she took my hands in hers. "It's Marshall Astor," she said. "He's had a horrible accident."

21

▲

consumption

The whole story came over the phone line in bits and pieces that night from neighbors and family friends. I sifted the truth out of rumor and exaggeration, and had a pretty good idea what happened.

Marshall Astor had taken his mother's car out for a joyride. He went speeding on bald tires and lost control on a bridge, halfway across the river—the same bridge where his father had gone sailing off into oblivion. The county, however, had reinforced the guardrails after his father's accident, so instead of crashing into the river, Marshall ended up with a smashed front end, a deployed air bag, and an unspecified number of broken bones. Although everyone called it an "accident," and a "coincidence" that it happened to be on the same bridge, I don't think there was anything accidental about it . . . And I don't think Marshall ever once lost control of that car.

I went to visit him the next evening, after he got home from the hospital. I wasn't sure what to expect from him, but I knew that I had to go.

His mother looked at me with frightened, distrustful eyes— like she might have looked at me when I was still ugly.

"Come in," she said. "Let me tell Marshall you're here."

I waited in the living room until Marshall rolled out in a wheelchair a few moments later. He had black eyes from the punch of the air bag against his face. Both of his ankles were in casts. The impact had broken them.

"Hi, Linda."

"Hi, Marshall."

As sweet as revenge had felt a few weeks before, it felt empty now. Empty and dark. Just by looking at him, I knew that I was really the one who had driven him off the bridge. He was in love. People in love do desperate things. My own responsibility in this was almost impossible to bear, because no matter how black my heart had become, it was still beating. No matter how deep a coma my conscience was in, it couldn't ignore this.

We sat there for a long time, not saying anything. I tried to look everywhere in the room but at him, and yet I kept being drawn back to his gaze.

"Why did you do it, Linda?" he finally said. "I loved you. Why did you do what you did?"

I thought about all the answers I could give him—or, more accurately, all the ways I could worm out of answering him. "It's complicated," I could tell him—or "We weren't right for each other." But I knew I owed him far more than an excuse.

"Why, Linda?" he asked again. And so I told him.

"Because my name isn't Linda. It's Cara."

His face went through a whole series of emotions. Disbelief, denial, and finally acceptance. All in about five seconds.

"Cara DeFido," he said, and repeated it, maybe just to make sure he heard himself right. "Cara DeFido."

I nodded. "I'm sorry." It was lame to say it now, but still, I had to do it.

As I watched him, I saw his face going red. He began to bite his lower lip, and tears began to flow from his eyes. Not just flow, but gush. "You had a good time that night, didn't you?"

"What?"

"The homecoming dance. I promised you'd have a good time, and you did, right? At least until I puked in the punch bowl."

He laughed the tiniest bit through his tears.

"I did have a good time," I admitted. "I wish I hadn't ruined it."

Marshall tried to wipe away his tears, but he didn't have much luck, because they just kept on coming. "I agreed to do it because of the car," he said. "I guess that makes me a creep."

I tried to put myself in his place. If someone offered me a car to go on a date with Tuddie—with *Aaron*—a few years ago, would I have done it? Even if I was the most popular girl in school? When it comes down to it, who wouldn't?

"I'm no one to judge," I told him.

"For what it's worth, I had a good time that night, too," he said. "I wasn't expecting to, but I did."

By now he had gotten his tears under control. He moved his legs and grimaced slightly. So I reached into my pocket and pulled out a small piece of paper. A paper that was woven from strands of swan gossamer.

"Here," I said, handing it to him. "Tear this in half, and slide a piece of it inside both of your casts," I said. "It will help you heal."

He rubbed it between his fingers. "Feels nice," he said. "What does 'find the answers' mean?"

"Nothing," I told him. "Nothing at all."

As I walked home from Marshall's that night, I felt dizzy, weak, and feverish. My head pounded, and it took all my strength just to make it home. Harmony had warned me of this. Why hadn't I listened?

"Did you see Marshall?" Momma asked as I came in. "How was he? Is he all right?"

"He'll be fine," I told her.

Then she took a good look at me. "Cara, are you feeling all right? You're not looking yourself."

I was afraid to think about what that meant. "I'm fine!" I pushed my way past her, went into my room, and tried to lock the door behind me, but this was one day that Momma wasn't giving me my privacy.

"Honey," she said, "what happened to Marshall isn't your fault. He's a troubled boy."

"He's a shallow boy," I told her. "He wasn't troubled until I came along to trouble him."

Momma smiled slightly. "Don't give yourself that much credit, dear. You may be beautiful now, but you're not Helen of Troy."

I lay down on my bed and thought about that. The face that launched a thousand ships. A woman who brought two empires into bloody battle. I wondered if Helen of Troy had been to the fountain herself.

"Momma," I asked, "did you like me more before? Has being beautiful made me horrible?"

"I love you the same either way."

I found it both comforting and unsettling. It was good to know I was loved before, but now I wanted to be loved *more*.

Momma sat down beside me and touched her hand to my forehead. "Cara, you're burning up."

"It's just exhaustion," I told her. "I'll sleep it off."

She looked doubtful, but she let me be, promising to check in on me during the night.

My body was aching, and I knew that whatever this illness was, it wasn't something that anyone could do anything about. I closed my eyes and felt myself falling into a troubled, fevered sleep, from which I was afraid I'd never wake up.

When I finally opened my eyes, I was in Abuelo's mansion, standing in his grand reflectorium—but Abuelo wasn't there. I was alone. Then I heard an unexpected voice.

I will make it my business to be there when your destiny comes calling.

It was Miss Leticia! I turned to see her right in the center of the room, seated at her little garden table, with a pot of tea.

"Come, child," she said. "Tea's waiting. Drink it before it gets cold."

"But . . . but you're dead."

Miss Leticia laughed and laughed. "Not so dead that we can't have a nice visit."

I sat across from her, knowing that this had to be a dream, but also knowing I wouldn't awake until we had had our little visit.

She poured a single cup of tea, but it was clear as water, and when I looked into the cup, it was swirling with colors, like the northern lights.

"Hurry," she said. "Drink your destiny before it's too late."

I picked up the cup and looked down into it, but the water

was gone. Instead it was full of mud. Mud swarming with worms. I tried to drop the cup, but my hands wouldn't move.

Miss Leticia sighed. "My, my, my," she said. "Will you look at that. Nothing more rancid than ruined destiny. Y'still gotta drink it, though—and the longer you wait, the worse it'll get."

Then she was gone, the wormy cup was gone, and I was alone, surrounded by Abuelo's many mirrors, reflecting my beautiful face.

One mirror wasn't beautiful, though. One mirror showed me the ugly girl I had once been. This dream mirror held that awful reflection and was strong enough not to break. Then a second mirror showed my old face, and a third. Soon half the mirrors showed me as I once was, while the other half showed what I looked like now. Slowly I walked toward one of the offensive mirrors, and with each step, I felt hotter and hotter, my fever growing—more than just fever, I felt anger as I looked at that horrible face.

"How dare you come back!" I told it. "After all I've been through, how dare you show your ugly face around here."

"There are worse things than being ugly," the nasty reflection said, but I wasn't going to listen to a thing it said. It had no control over me.

"I'm stronger than you!" I told it.

It didn't answer me—it just waited to see if I truly was. And so I closed my eyes and reached to the core of myself, pulling up all the strength I could muster.

It wasn't enough. I could feel myself losing the battle. I knew I had to pull strength from somewhere else, but how could I? Suddenly the answer came to me.

"I am not ugly!" I declared out loud. "Not inside, not out." And I began to summon strength from beyond myself.

"B-E-A-U-T-I-F-U-L."

Spells and spelling. Words. *My* words. They had the power.

"R-A-V-I-S-H-I-N-G."

I could feel strength coming to me now. I was drawing it from the room around me!

"S-P-L-E-N-D-I-F-E-R-O-U-S."

Beyond the room, I was tapping into the earth itself.

"G-L-O-R-I-O-U-S."

It felt like flood waters spilling into an empty vessel.

"G-R-A-C-E-F-U-L."

A powerful energy filled me, and when I was full to the brim, I opened my eyes. Then I spelled my final word to my hideous reflections.

"D—"

I pushed the ugliness away with all the force of my soul, and—

"I—"

—one by one those mirrors changed, until every face I saw was a face of absolute beauty.

"E!"

A beautiful face everywhere I looked. I had killed the ugliness. I had won! I had won!

I woke to the grating sound of my alarm clock, and turned it off. It was morning, and my fever was gone. There was a stench in the air, though. It was faint, it was foul, and I couldn't quite place it.

I got out of bed and did what I always did since the day I'd gotten back. I caught my gaze in my mirror, tossed my hair until it fell into perfect place, smiled that million-dollar smile. I thought about the dream. No cup of worms for me! I had beaten the illness, Marshall would recover, I would get over Gerardo. Things would be fine. I went out to join my family for breakfast.

The smell was worse in the rest of the house, reminding me of the roadkill that had once filled my room. "What is that god-awful stench?" I asked as I walked into the kitchen.

"What stench, dear?" Momma said.

She was at the sink, washing dishes, and Vance had his nose in the refrigerator. Only Dad was sitting down, the paper open wide in front of him.

So I sat down across from him, and when Dad lowered the newspaper, what I saw made me scream.

At the sound, Momma dropped a glass, and it crashed on the floor.

"Cara! What in God's name?"

Exactly what I thought. *What in God's name?* Because the face before me was not the one I'd known yesterday. My father's teeth, always a little bit yellow, were practically green now, and twisted in his head like tilted tombstones in a forgotten grave-yard. His nose hooked miserably to one side. And he had a Ne-anderthal ridge on his forehead.

I looked at Momma for an explanation, but what I saw there was even worse. Hollow gray cheeks, eyes too close and sunk deep in their sockets, a dangling piece of skin on her neck like a turkey, and tufts of blond hair so thin you could see her pink peeling scalp.

I gasped and put my hand over my mouth to keep from screaming again.

Nothing more rancid than ruined destiny.

"Honey, you don't look right," said Momma. "Have you still got a fever?"

I could only shake my head. How could I begin to explain?

When Vance turned to me, I wasn't looking at my brother. What stared back at me from the fridge looked more like a rat than a human being. Those front teeth of his that had always had the slightest of overbites now stuck so far out of his mouth he couldn't get his lips around them.

"What's up with her?"

"Look at yourselves!" I shouted. "Don't you see?"

Momma turned to Dad. She squinted her sunken eyes and said, "Honey, you really should shave before you go off to the car lot."

"Shave?" I said. *"Shave?!"*

I stood up, and the chair behind me fell over.

"You gonna eat that waffle?" said the rat boy in my brother's clothes.

I bolted out of there, running through a trailer park twice as decrepit as it had been the day before. What was it that kept them from seeing the change in one another? I couldn't explain it any more than I could explain the transformational power of the fountain. Then I thought of my dad, and his old TV shows. Strange hair, ugly clothes, weird talk, all of which had been perfectly normal in a certain time and place.

Is that what had happened just now? Did my parents and my brother come to see this new ugliness as normal, instantly getting used to it, just as they had gotten so used to that horrible stench that filled the air?

That stench!

I was out of the trailer park now, and in a neighborhood of once-beautiful homes. But now the well-tended yards were choked with weeds, and the pavement was cracked and pushing up at awkward angles. The homes had a sagging sadness that nothing short of a bulldozer could repair. The smell kept growing stronger, and now a buzzing sound filled the air as well.

Then, when I rounded a corner, I saw where the sound and the smell were coming from.

Vista View Cemetery.

There were flowers on the hillside of Vista View. Miss Leticia's roses and ferns had all dried up and died . . . but one flower had gone to seed. What was it Miss Leticia had said? That the sweet and the rancid both have their place in the world? But what happens when the sweetness is drained away?

Now covering the hill were dozens upon dozens of corpse flowers. Big, huge, brown petals around oozing stalks. I recognized the buzzing as the sound of a million flies, swarming around the massive blooms, practically blackening the sky.

I covered my nose, my mouth; I tried not to breathe. I turned in the other direction, running away from it, but there were fresh seedlings in every yard—maybe only six inches tall now, but growing. According to Miss Leticia, the foul plant took three years to bloom—but ugliness now had its own timetable. The way scar tissue filled a wound, something had to fill the space left when what little beauty this town had had was sucked away.

Sucked away by me.

It began with Marisol. I had taken her looks by force, so it happened in an instant—but the rest of the town had faded slowly—too slowly for me to really see at first. I was too busy looking in the mirror to notice. Then came the illness—and I now understood the vision I had had during my fevered dream. Harmony had warned me, but I hadn't understood.

Consumption.

What a perfect name for this strange illness—because in the throes of fever, something was most definitely consumed. *The fire of beauty now burns within you,* Abuelo had told me. It *was* a fire . . . and like every fire, it needed to be fueled. There in De León, the fountain didn't just give us beauty, it fueled it. The water was in the grass, in the trees, in the very air of the valley. But once I left, the flame of beauty had to find its fuel elsewhere. I suppose if my will had been weaker, the flame would have died. My face would have sagged, my ugliness would have returned. But that didn't happen. I was strong, and my beauty was predatory. And so in the depth of my fever, I began to steal beauty around me, consuming it like a wildfire in the wind. Consuming it like . . . a black hole. My face now truly *was* a black hole, draining away the beauty of anything that came too close.

Just how far did this go? Was it just the neighborhood around the trailer park—or did it go farther? There was only one way to find out.

I ignored the awful stench and unsightly visions around me, and I stumbled my way across the jagged, root-cracked pavement of my ruined town until I reached school.

22

gauntlet of grunge

The beige bricks of Flock's Rest High had gone black, as though they'd been covered in soot. Grime filled the corners of every window. The flagpole leaned like the mast of a sunken ship, and the flag that waved there was tattered and twisted.

If I'd had any doubts, they were gone as I walked through the halls of my school. Every face I saw was grotesque and stomach churning, and I wondered if after today there would be any mirrors left intact in town. Then I came around a bank of lockers and found myself staring into the bulging eyes of the one person I never wanted to see again.

Marisol Yeager.

Her exile hadn't lasted long. She was back with her friends, laughing, talking, smiling with teeth so gray they could have been made of asphalt. When she saw me, she became quiet. They all became quiet.

"Well, look who's here," she said. "The Flock's Rest Monster."

Her clothes, which had always been so pretty, were a wild mishmash of colors and textures.

"I'm sorry," I told Marisol. I never thought I'd say that to her. And even if I said it, I never thought I'd mean it. I looked at the freak show of faces all around me. "I'm sorry. This is not what I wanted. I never meant to make you all so . . . so . . . ugly."

They looked at me and at one another, not understanding what I was talking about—except for Marisol. She knew who I was; she knew what I had done. Maybe she couldn't explain it, but she knew.

"Hasn't anyone told you?" she said, with a nasty gray-mouthed smile. "Ugly is the new pretty."

Her words left a mark on my mind just as black as the ink stain I had left on her blouse. I wanted to scream, but it came out as a weak warble. I ran for the nearest exit—but as I neared the doors, the school security guard stepped in my way. He scowled at me with a face that was little more than a bloated pustule. "Where do you think you're going?" he said. "Get to class."

With every exit guarded, I was trapped within this pageant of monstrosities.

How do you judge beauty? They say beauty is in the eye of the beholder, but that's not true. Beauty is in the spirit of the world in which you live. It's where your world *tells* you it is—the beholder has no choice in the matter . . . and if your world finds beauty in the black pit of ugliness, then that's where your beauty lies. *Ugly is the new pretty*. The thought followed me through the rest of that horrible day. For the people of Flock's Rest, it wasn't just their faces and bodies that had changed, but the yardstick by which they judged.

At lunch, I found myself at a table alone. Sure, there were others there to start with, but bit by bit they drifted away. Everything was back to the way it had been before. I was the only beautiful girl in town—and yet I was alone, untouchable, while all around me kids with the faces of ghouls laughed and enjoyed themselves.

I was so lost in my thoughts, I hadn't realized someone had sat down at the table—and when I looked up, there was Gerardo in the mercy seat.

"Hi," he said.

Gerardo hadn't been spared. He was just as repulsive as everyone else. I didn't want to accept that I had done this to him. "Things didn't turn out the way I wanted."

"They never do," he said.

"You do see what's happened, don't you? No one else seems to notice—but you must see it."

And then he shrugged. "Yeah. You get used to it, though."

"Used to it? But how do you get used to *this*?" I grabbed his ear that looked more like a cauliflower. "And this?" I grabbed his chin, which stuck out unevenly from his face.

He smacked my hand away. "Some things give a face character, all right? I don't expect you to understand that. Your face is just creamy smooth. No character to it. All right, I'll admit it: I thought that new face of yours was pretty for a while—but now when I look at you, it doesn't do a thing for me. It's like looking at a bowl of sugar. Sure, it's sweet. But it's got no flavor."

"Why'd you come over here, Gerardo?"

"To warn you," he said. He looked to the door of the cafeteria, and now when I glanced around, I could see that most of the kids had cleared out, even though the bell hadn't rung. "They're planning something," he told me. "I thought you should know. And I wanted you to know that I had nothing to do with it."

"But you're not going to stop it, either."

He shook his head. "No, I'm not."

Then he took my hand and gently placed into my palm a sliver of broken glass. It was the piece of the mirror I had broken for him. The piece he said he would keep forever.

"Good-bye, Cara."

When I stepped out of the cafeteria, I was faced with a gathering of dozens of kids. They stood on either side of the hallway, waiting for me to pass between them. At the far end was the exit, wide open and waiting, with no guard or teachers in sight.

I strode forward, and felt something soft and wet hit my shoulder. A rotten strawberry. Then something else hit my back. I looked down to see a moldy orange on the floor.

In an instant, it became a storm. I was pelted from all angles by rotten fruit, rancid meat, and containers of sour milk that exploded on me like water balloons. Someone hurled a rotten melon, which burst painfully upon my chest—but I weathered this storm, walking forward, holding my head high against the gauntlet of grunge, until I finally reached the end of the hall, where their chief conspirator stood between me and the door.

"You've never been one of us," said Marisol. "You'll never *be* one of us . . . and you don't belong here."

She held in her hand an onion, spotted green from mildew, soft, slimy, and dripping. She hefted it in her hand, ready to hurl it at my face, but then she said, "You know what? I'm not gonna waste this on you." And then she lifted the onion to her mouth and took a big, healthy bite.

To this day, I can still smell that putrid onion on her breath when she said, "Get out."

23

▲

THE UGLY PLACES

Harmony had been right. Aaron had been right. There was no place for me in the outside world, and there were worse things than being ugly. I should have known what would happen when I left, but I was too headstrong to realize the truth. I doubted Flock's Rest would ever return to the way it had been. Everyone there was cursed to the kind of ugliness that shattered mirrors.

The true curse was not with them, however. I was the one cursed. I was a thief of beauty, and the only place I could ever live in peace was De León. The ghetto for those too beautiful for this world.

For weeks, I had blocked out my thoughts of De León. I had chosen not to think about anything or anyone there, but now those thoughts and feelings came flooding back. I missed everyone—but most of all I missed Aaron. After all he had done for me, I had chosen to abandon him. That was as cruel as what I had done to Marshall. He didn't deserve that! I didn't know if he'd ever forgive me, but I knew once I'd made it back, I'd have an eternity to make it up to him.

I didn't feel the pull this time, as I had when I'd first left town, but I knew where to go. I walked, my feet aching in my shoes. By dusk, the wind had shifted and the smell of corpse flower faded. I walked until my feet were blistered. I didn't get offered any rides. I didn't look in the windows of any passing cars, for fear of the face I might see. I took a heavy coat from the coatrack in a roadside diner once night fell, and kept on walking well past midnight. I allowed myself only a few hours to sleep in the shelter of a sad, abandoned barn that looked even older and more abandoned at dawn.

Just like Harmony, I was now wiser than when I left. Just like Harmony, I had gained that wisdom the hard way. Abuelo had accepted her back, hadn't he? He would accept me back as well; I had to believe it, because it was the only thing that kept me going.

A few hours later, I finally found what I was looking for. The fading billboard with my mother's Cadillac and her smiling face, from the days when she and Dad were happy, and their lives were full of hope.

DEFIDO MOTORS, WHERE FINS STAND FOR STATUS.

My mere presence made the faint image fade into nothingness. Gray peeling paint against gray warping wood.

The path behind the billboard was overgrown, but it was still there. I took that path, climbing the foothills until those hills got steeper and turned into mountains. They weren't the kind of mountains you need heavy equipment to climb, but they were steep enough to make the process slow and exhausting. I was at the end of my endurance, but it wasn't muscles that drove me now. It was the knowledge that soon I'd be among the beautiful people of De León. Soon I would be home.

The air was colder and thinner the higher I climbed, until I saw in the distance, on a hill just a few miles away, a white stone building. I knew it was the monastery that Aaron had spoken of.

Turn west when you see the monastery, he had said.

I hiked through the night, stumbling, bruising, but never stopping. Scaling these treacherous hillsides in the dark was a dangerous thing. I could have slipped and broken my neck at any time, and put an end to my fragile eternessence—but I found I didn't care. *De León or death,* I told myself with every step. *De León or death.*

Then, finally, at dawn, I came to the valley. I knew, because I recognized the yellowed hillside and the bald spot where the monks picked up the weekly garbage.

I took only a moment to rest and breathe in my relief at finally being home. *Where should I go first?* I thought. *Should I find Aaron?* That's what I wanted to do, but I decided that I needed to pay respect where respect was due. My first stop would be Abuelo's mansion. I would bow before him. No—I would get down on my knees and beg for his forgiveness. I would cry, sincere tears of repentance, and the anguish of a lesson painfully learned.

There, there, Abuelo would say. *No tears here in the valley. The Caldero sheds all the tears we need—and they are all tears of joy.* He would touch my chin, and I would look into his handsome, ancient eyes, and he would smile. *Welcome home, Cara,* he would say. *Now come and create our own sweet language.*

The valley stretched out before me, hidden beneath a blanket of low, soft clouds. Filled with a joy I hadn't felt since before I left, I descended the hillside, into the cloud bank.

When I emerged from the clouds, the rest of the valley was there before me . . . but something was very wrong. This was still the town of De León, but it was not the way I remembered.

The hills that had been so gloriously green when I had left were now the color of mud, and the beautiful homes were no longer white. In fact, they seemed not to have any paint on them at all.

As I got closer I could see the warping, aged wood of each building, as gray as the homes I had left behind in Flock's Rest. The gazebo in the center of the beautiful park had fallen apart.

I couldn't catch my breath. I couldn't believe what I was seeing. Decay had crept into this beautiful valley so quickly, it looked like it had been abandoned for decades.

"Hello!" I called out. "Aaron! Harmony! Anybody!"

But no one was there to hear me. The town was deserted. At the far end of the stone path, Abuelo's mansion was gone. It had burned to the ground, and all that remained were black cinders and the charred memory of beams.

Then, as the clouds lifted just a bit, I saw the hillside above the ruined mansion, and my heart, as sick as it was, found a glimmer of hope—because there, high on the hill, was a patch of green!

It was near the spot where Aaron and I had picnicked, at the entrance to the cave that led to the fountain.

Of course, I thought to myself, *that's where they've all gone. The fountain must be fading, and they've all gone down there to nurture it.*

With renewed strength, I climbed to the plateau. The grass there was yellowing, but for every yellow blade, there was still a blade of green. There was still beauty here.

I found the entrance to the cave, stumbled in the darkness until I found a torch and matches to light it. Then, following the path Aaron and I had taken once before, I wended my way down, down, down, into the heart of the mountain, where the air was stale and hot.

I heard no skittering sounds of creatures around me this time, and as I neared the cavern Abuelo called the Cauldron of Life, I got a sinking feeling in the pit of my soul.

Because I didn't hear any voices.

When I finally came to the great cavern, the truth hit me as hard and as heavy as my first sight of the dead valley.

There was nobody here. It was without question the loneliest moment of my life.

The cavern itself was as dark as any other, with no gentle shimmering glow from the stones. The only light came from my torch. The place was dead. Panic welled up inside me. It locked my joints in place, and there were no words I could spell that could push me forward. In the end, it was the fear of my torch burning out that got me moving.

As I neared the dangling stalactite, and the stone basin into which the fountain had dripped, I saw something white on the ground in front of it.

It was a dress. *My* dress, folded into a perfect square, its swan-gossamer fabric shimmering with the light of my torch. It was the only hint of the beauty that had once been here.

On top of it was the ink brush they had made for me, and a letter with my name on it.

Sticking my torch into the dying, mulchy ground, I knelt down and opened the letter. The handwriting was not the sweeping flourishes of Abuelo's hand. It was Aaron's handwriting.

> *Dear Cara,*
>
> *It's been two weeks since you left. Where are you? Harmony says something must have happened, that maybe they didn't let you leave Flock's Rest. Or worse, that you died on your way there or*

back—but I won't let myself believe it. You can't imagine how much I miss you—and how frightened I am for you.

The fountain is drying up. Everything around us is dying. Abuelo says not to worry, that he senses in his bones where the fountain is going next, and everyone says he's always been right before. He won't tell us where we're headed, but he does say to prepare for a long journey. We've been bottling water from the fountain to take with us. Enough to last us until we get to wherever we're going. He's furious at you for leaving, Cara—but I know if you come back to us, he'll forgive you. Abuelo never stays angry for long.

The monks have already left to prepare our way, so I'm leaving this by the fountain, because it's the only place I know for sure you'll look. We leave tomorrow at dawn, but I'm not giving up hope. Wherever we go, I'll be waiting for you. Find us, Cara.

Love always,
Aaron

My tears wet the pages and the ink began to run. Carefully, I folded the letter and put it in my pocket, took my Aaron-hair brush, my dress, and picked up the torch.

Clinging to the slim hope that Abuelo was wrong, I held the torch high to see the tip of the stalactite—maybe there was still life dripping into the fountain, and they'd all come back. But as glistening wet as the stalactite had been before, it was now dry as a bone. In the basin beneath it, there was a single spot of moisture. I reached toward it with my finger, but even as I did, the moisture was sucked up by the stone. Then the basin cracked and started to crumble.

I stepped back, and I felt the ground around me begin to shake. Little bits of stone fell from above. Sensing what was coming, I leaped back, but not quickly enough. The massive stalactite broke off from the cavern roof and crashed to the ground, shattering into a million pieces, burying me beneath the rubble.

I was bruised and battered, but not broken.

I picked up my torch, which was almost out, fanned it until it was full flame again, and made my way back to the surface.

They had left without me.

I could have been with them, if only I had kept my promise and returned. The truth of it hurt more than the cuts and bruises from the fallen stalactite, and I cried until there were no tears left inside me, and my eyes went as dry as the ruined fountain.

I stepped out of the cave, into the light of a gray day, and stood there on the plateau, desperately trying to get a sense of direction. Where had they gone? Back when the fountain had been strong, I'd been able to feel it pulling me, coaxing me up in the middle of the night, leaving me facing northwest—but that was when the fountain was close by. Perhaps Abuelo could still feel it in his bones, but I wasn't Abuelo. I felt no pull, no gravity, no sense of direction at all. Wherever the fountain had gone, it was out of my reach.

As I stood there, I watched as the last of the green grass turned yellow, then brown.

And in my hands, my beautiful dress, woven from the gossamer down of swans, disintegrated into strands that blew away like cobwebs in the wind.

"Hello, pretty lady."

I didn't go back the way I came. Instead I continued west

across the mountains and ended up at the same gas station where I had first been dropped with the garbage. Now the same gangly gas-station attendant greeted me. Greasy hands, goat hair sticking out of his Adam's apple, but right there, right then, he seemed like Prince Charming.

"Second time I seen you here with no car," he said. "I'm startin' to think you're just comin' to see me!"

And as I looked at him I thought, *This boy is not so bad.* I could find a place for myself in this tiny rest stop of a town. He wasn't Aaron. He wasn't even Marshall or Gerardo. But after what I had left behind, I would rather take dumb and homely over bleak and hideous any day.

Then, to my horror, I quickly came to realize that there would be no rest for me here, or anywhere else . . . because as I looked at him, I could see the features of his face already beginning to change. His Adam's apple, already large, started to bulge forward like a buzzard's neck, the hairs in his nose began to grow, curling outward—and I knew if I stayed here any length of time at all, it would be Flock's Rest all over again. This place would just become a creepy roadside attraction where no one would dare stop, even for gas.

He smiled at me, and I swear I could see his teeth starting to twist out of line. "Look at you," he said. "I do believe you're getting prettier by the second!"

I backed away from him quickly.

"I can't stay," I said. "I've got to get out of this place. I've got to get out now!"

"Suit yourself," he said. "The Greyhound bus stops at the Denny's down the road a bit. You can still make it if you hurry."

And so I did. Scrounging together what money I had in my pockets, and what money I could beg from people coming in and out of Denny's, I got myself bus fare and rode that bus as far as it would take me.

That was a long time ago. I've been riding ever since, crisscrossing the country, zigzagging the world, searching for a hint of where they might have gone. My only belongings are the clothes on my back, a journal in which I write the words of a new language that no one has yet to speak, and the brush I use to write them, made from the hair of my one true love.

I will find them.

They could be anywhere. It's a big world to cover—but I've got an eternity to do it. It may take me a thousand years, but I will find them.

Until then, I will ride buses, and stow away on trains, and steal plane fare as I weave my way through the world, leaving every place a little less beautiful with my passing—although I may catch the faces of my fellow passengers when they get on board, I won't dare look at the monstrosities they've become once they get off.

So if, by chance, your travels happen to leave you seated beside the most beautiful girl in the world, don't ask questions, don't make small talk—just leave your luggage, tear up your ticket, and run.

Because I am one of the beautiful people, and my beauty is the blackest of holes.

Don't make me spell it out for you.